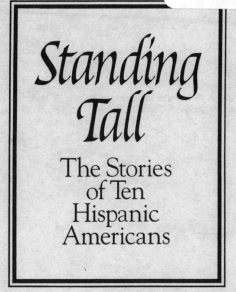

Standing Tall

The Stories of Ten Hispanic Americans

by Argentina Palacios

RETURN to ESL library
J. EICHENOUR

SCHOLASTIC INC.
New York Toronto London Auckland Sydney

Cover and Interior Photo Credits

Gloria Estefan courtesy of UPI/Bettmann. Roberto Clemente courtesy of
UPI/Bettmann. Dr. Antonia C. Novello courtesy of Dr. Antonia C. Novello.
Fernando Bujones courtesy of Martha Swope © 1987. Miriam Santos cour-
tesy of Miriam Santos. Franklin R. Chang-Díaz courtesy of The Bettmann
Archive. Vilma S. Martínez courtesy of Vilma S. Martínez. Jaime Esca-
lante courtesy of AP/Wide World Photos. Dr. Severo Ochoa courtesy of
AP/Wide World. Admiral David G. Farragut courtesy of Wide World
Photos.

ISBN 0-590-47140-6

Copyright © 1994 by Argentina Palacios.
All rights reserved. Published by Scholastic Inc.

24 23 22 21 20 19 18 17 16   5 6 7 8 9/0

Printed in the U.S.A.   40

First Scholastic printing, November 1994

To Howard Goodkin,
for the immense work he did in his short life
so Hispanic children can stand tall and proud.

Acknowledgments

Thanks to all those who made this book possible: my husband, Samuel Ziegler, who helped me research, read every word of the manuscript, and made valuable suggestions; my editor, Ann Reit, who suggested the writing of this book; my agent, Liza Pulitzer Voges, who gave me advice. Others whose help is greatly appreciated are Jeanne and Robert Lindsay, Herlinda and Robert Saitz, Didier T. Jaén, Guillermo Ellerbrock, Stanley Simmons, NASA, MALDEF, and the Ford Foundation.

To the subjects profiled in this book who graciously agreed to an interview, a million thanks. To those subjects who are no longer with us, thanks for the pleasure of researching their lives.

The services of the Queens Borough Public Library, the New York Public Library, the Brooklyn Public Library, the St. John's University Main Library and Law Library, the Hispanic Division of the Library of Congress, were invaluable for the completion of this book. Thanks to these and other libraries for making a writer's work easier.

Contents

Introduction

The 1990 U.S. census counted 22.4 million people who identified themselves as "Hispanic." Some Hispanic organizations think that this figure is too low. They believe there are many more who for one reason or another were not counted. Even without any increase, the 1990 census indicates that Hispanics are the second largest ethnic minority in the United States. Soon after the beginning of the twenty-first century, according to some estimates, Hispanics will be the largest.

The influence of things Hispanic is undeniable in California, Texas, New Mexico, Arizona, and Colorado. But it is also felt in the Northeast, the Midwest, and the Northwest, and in our newest states. In Alaska, there is a large concentration of Hispanics working in the fish canning industry. In Hawaii, due to the large number of Hispanics, there are local cable TV programs in Spanish.

Today, Hispanics are found doing the unsung stoop labor of the migrant workers who toil in the fields that give us food. They are also found in outer space where only the most highly trained few can explore. Hispanics contribute to life in the United States in every possible occupation.

This book highlights Hispanics from various fields. There are many individuals worthy of consideration. Every reader of this book could probably make a selection totally different from this one, and just as inspiring. From a nineteenth-century naval hero to a pop music idol of today, the ones profiled here are truly outstanding individuals.

A few explanations about terms. Some prefer the word Latino to refer to people, born in the United States or Latin America, who have Spanish-speaking ancestors. But, in reality, Latino applies to everyone in Latin America, including the Portuguese-speaking Brazilians. The term Hispanic refers to people with ancestors who can be traced back to Spain. This book includes people with that one Spanish tie, wherever they were born. That's why Hispanic is used in this book more often than Latino.

In truth, however, "Hispanics" or "Latinos" are more likely to call themselves Mexicans, Puerto Ricans, Cubans, Dominicans, Panamanians, Argentinians, etc. Some people of Mexican descent may use the term Mexican-American; others prefer Chicano.

There are similarities among the people and cultures in Hispanic groups, but they are not exactly alike. It would be like comparing people from Wisconsin and people from Louisiana — some things they have in common, some things they don't. The people in this book come from a variety of backgrounds within that larger Hispanic community. They have done or are doing their most productive work in the United States. They are real people with virtues and defects but they all stand tall.

1

David G. Farragut

Far from the land of his Spanish ancestors, a boy was born in Stony Point, also called Campbell's Station, Tennessee, at the very edge of the wilderness. In due time, he was to make history.

Born on July 5, 1801, James Glasgow Farragut, usually called Glasgow by his family, was the second child of George Farragut and his wife, the former Elizabeth Shine. His mother's family moved from North Carolina to Tennessee when she was very young. His father, named Jorge Antonio Magin Ferragut at birth, the son of Antonio Ferragut and Juana Mesquida, was from Minorca, one of the Balearic Islands, off the east coast of Spain. Some books spell the family name Ferregut, but in Spain and Latin America the name is spelled Ferragut.

It is not clear when and why the name Jorge

Ferragut changed to George Farragut. On the blank page of a Bible owned by the family of the younger Farragut, the following inscription was written by hand:

My Son: Your father, George Farragut, was born in the island of Minorca, in the Mediterranean, in 1755, the 29th of September, in Ciudadela, and came away from that Island the 2d day of April, 1772 — came to America in March, 1776. Your mother, Elizabeth Shine, was born in North Carolina, Dobbs Co., near Kinsston on the Neuse River, in 1765, on the 7th of June. Her father, John Shine — mother, Ellenor McIven.

George Farragut made sure his children knew the Spanish language, and taught them about their illustrious family, which included several centuries of bishops, councilors, and scholars. In the Middle Ages, one of his forebears, Don Pedro Ferragut, fought heroically by the side of King James I of Aragón. He was Sargent before the King, an office of high honor and importance, held only by those of noble blood. Another notable in the family tree, Captain Antonio Ferragut, served with distinction in the Spanish Navy during the reign of King Philip IV, in the sixteen hundreds.

George Farragut went to sea at the age of ten, sailing in merchant ships. In 1775 he came to New Orleans and heard that the American colonies were unhappy with Great Britain. Adventure was in the air, so he decided to join the revolutionary forces.

George Farragut served in the South Carolina Navy and the Continental Army, rising to the rank of major of the cavalry. At the end of the conflict, he settled in Tennessee and became an officer in the militia guarding the frontier. It was there that he married, in 1795, and started a family.

In 1803, in what is known as the Louisiana Purchase, the United States bought from France a vast amount of territory that extended from the Mississippi River to the Rocky Mountains, and from the Gulf of Mexico to Canada. The Farraguts moved to Louisiana, where George Farragut got a commission and was stationed at the naval base in New Orleans. He left Tennessee first and later on, his wife, a woman as self-reliant as her husband, sailed with the children to meet him. The family made its home on the banks of Lake Pontchartrain. George Farragut frequently took the youngsters sailing, regardless of the weather. *When anyone suggested to him the risk to which he subjected his children in thus crossing the lake, he generally replied that "now was the time to conquer their fears,"* wrote his son about those excursions.

In 1808, while fishing on Lake Pontchartrain, George Farragut found an old man, prostrated by sunstroke, in another fishing boat. The gentleman was David Porter, a navy man Farragut knew. He took Porter to his nearby home and he and Eliz-

abeth Farragut nursed him for an extended period, but he never recovered. During that time,
Elizabeth Farragut suddenly became ill with yellow fever, then a common affliction in the
swampy areas of the Mississippi region. She died
shortly afterward, and she and David Porter were
buried on the same day.

By this time, the oldest Farragut boy, William,
had joined the U.S. Navy. George Farragut still
had four other children to raise by himself —
Glasgow, George, Jr., Nancy, and baby Elizabeth.
Life was not easy for them.

One day, in 1809, a young man in dashing uniform came to visit. He was the son of David Porter. Like his father, he was a naval officer, and he
was also named David Porter. When his father
had died, the young Porter had been at sea. He
now came to thank the Farraguts for their
kindness.

Commander David Porter told George Farragut
that he and his wife would like to help him. Later
on they would have ten children, but at that time,
the Porters had none. He told Farragut they
would like to raise one of the Farragut children.
It was a hard decision for George to make, and
the matter was discussed with the children. Glasgow made the decision for himself: "I, being in-
spired by his uniform and that of my brother
William, who had received an appointment in the
navy some time before, said promptly that I
would go." He lived with the Porters in New Orleans but visited his father and siblings often,

crossing Lake Pontchartrain to a plantation on the Pascagoula River where they now made their home.

New Orleans was a bustling and exciting city with the Spanish, French, and Creole cultures mixing easily in its midst. There were thousands of people within its boundaries, more than the young boy had ever seen in the rural areas he knew. The Mississippi River was a watery highway. Commerce — legal as well as illegal — was the order of the day. Ships from Europe and Central and South America made it a port of call. Pirates, including the notorious brothers Jean and Pierre Laffite, made themselves at home in the area. James Glasgow Farragut accompanied Commander Porter on some pirate-tracking missions along the Mississippi. All of this was quite exciting for an eight-year-old boy. As he put it, "I soon became fond of this adventurous sort of life."

Before he turned nine, Farragut went along with Commander Porter on a business trip to Washington, D.C. Aboard the *Vesuvius*, they first sailed to Havana, Cuba. Commander Porter went to claim a $60,000 reward offered by the Spanish government for the capture of three pirate ships. These ships, the *Montebello*, the *Petite Chance*, and the *Intrepid*, disguised as privateers, were raiding Spanish possessions. Porter had captured all three in the Gulf of Mexico area.

In Cuba, young Farragut, who knew Spanish, heard stories of the British taking American seamen by force to fight for Britain. This was done

on the pretense that the men they took had been
born in England. There was much talk about the
U.S. brig *Vixen*, how it had been fired on by a
British warship. In later years, Farragut would
write: *This was the first thing that caused in me
bad feelings toward the English nation. I was too
young to know anything about the revolution; but
I looked upon this as an insult to be paid in kind,
and was anxious to discharge the debt with interest.*

Commander Porter was now stationed in
Washington, D.C. Mrs. Porter moved there and
they enrolled the young boy in school. Shortly
thereafter, Porter introduced the nine-year-old
James Glasgow to Paul Hamilton, the Secretary
of the Navy. The self-assured young Farragut
asked Secretary Hamilton for a commission in
the U.S. Navy. It was normal in those days for
young boys to join the navy as midshipmen —
but they were usually fourteen or fifteen. Nonetheless, the secretary was taken with James Glasgow's candor and eagerness. Porter indicated that
his foster son was a "regular river rat." Hamilton
promised the youngster a commission for his
tenth birthday and he kept his word, but the war-
rant arrived early, when the boy was nine-and-
a-half. It was dated December 17, 1810. The papers were issued in the name of David Glasgow
Farragut. Porter had given his foster son his
own first name, which Farragut used for the rest
of his life, and his signature was always "D.G.
Farragut."

David G. Farragut became the youngest person

who ever enlisted in the U.S. Navy, a record that stands no chance of being broken. Nowadays, no one can enlist before age seventeen.

The Porter family moved to Chester, Pennsylvania, Mrs. Porter's hometown. David Glasgow attended school in Chester until his guardian found the right moment to take him to sea under his watchful eyes.

That moment came in August 1811, when David was ten. Commander Porter and the young midshipman joined the frigate *Essex* in Norfolk, Virginia. Their assignment was to guard the coast, as part of a larger squadron, from marauding British ships. In the *Essex*, his home for the next three years, Midshipman Farragut learned the tools of his trade.

In July 1812, shortly after the U.S. Congress formally declared war on England, Porter, now promoted to captain, was given a new assignment.

At that time, there were many causes of friction between England and its former American colonies. Some people in the U.S. wanted to expand their country all the way to Canada. Canada was an English territory and the British were at war with France. British ships continuously raided U.S. merchant ships for supplies and manpower. The small new United States was too weak to put a stop to that practice. The U.S. Navy fleet consisted of 16 warships while the British fleet had 600. England, the great naval power, in fact, did as it pleased, flaunting its might. It violated international law and the freedom of the seas at will. It blockaded the American coast.

For a time, the American warships were kept in port. This way they were protected by the forts that dotted the coast. The job of the *Essex* and a few other similar ships was to break the blockade and attack British ships wherever they found them at sea.

The *Essex* accomplished its task. In two months it captured eight British merchant ships. Unarmed freighters could do nothing but surrender to a fully equipped warship.

In August 1812, the *Essex* spotted the British war sloop *Alert*, with all its guns mounted on the deck. The *Essex*, a frigate, with guns mounted on a lower level as well, flew the British flag to trick the *Alert*. When the *Alert* came closer to greet the ship, Captain Porter made the *Essex* turn, as if fleeing, and readied the guns. The *Alert* was now behind them. In the *Essex*, the British flag was taken down, and the U.S. flag raised. The British fired at the Americans, but the *Alert* was badly positioned and the shells did no damage to the *Essex*. Now it was Porter's turn to bombard. The *Alert* was forced to signal for surrender.

The crew of the *Essex* kept the *Alert* in tow and left its crewmen in their ship, but the officers were brought on board the *Essex* as prisoners. Soon the British prisoners were planning to take command of the *Essex*.

Late one night, young Farragut was lying in his hammock on the gun deck. He felt someone standing near him in the darkness. Before his barely opened eyes stood a British officer with a pistol in his hand. Farragut pretended to be asleep and the man went away without touching him. As soon as he considered it safe, the midshipman crept to Captain Porter's quarters and told him what had just happened. The captain rushed on deck and cried out, "Fire! Fire!" He knew this would work.

The crewmen of the *Essex* were used to fire drills. They took their positions calmly and orderly. The British, however, were in a great state of confusion and panic, thinking there was indeed a fire on board. They didn't know where to turn, and it was easy to get hold of them. Porter ordered the British prisoners locked in the ship's hold.

David Farragut's first heroic act at sea, at age eleven, saved the ship and its entire crew that night.

After ten weeks of action, the government ordered a complete refitting of the *Essex*. The ship sailed up the Delaware River in September and remained there until October.

Early in October, the *Essex* received orders to join a squadron that would cruise the Pacific Ocean in search of British merchant ships. In order to avoid British warships, the squadron would take a long and roundabout way. Porter sailed for the Cape Verde Islands, off the west coast of Africa, to rendezvous with the other ships of the squadron, which were coming from different ports. The *Essex* waited five days in the area

but the vessels never showed. This meant that the
captain was free to follow his own course, and
Porter headed for South America.

Crossing the Atlantic Ocean alone in those hostile days was a dangerous undertaking for an
unescorted ship. Fortunately, the *Essex* did not
meet any enemy warship. But it did meet a British ship carrying cargo, mail, and $55,000 in hard
currency. In war, it was fair and customary to
keep the bounty. The *Essex* waited for the rest of
the squadron at the next rendezvous point, the
island of Fernando de Noronha, off the coast of
Brazil, but the vessels were not seen there, either.

Captain Porter decided to proceed with the
original plan of sailing the Pacific, even though
his ship was alone and the weather around Cape
Horn was terrible at that time of year. At the tip
of South America, fierce gales of wind, angry de-
structive waves, and violent storms thrashed the
little *Essex* for twenty-one days. More than once
the men thought the ship would sink. Farragut
later wrote about the experience: *This was the
only instance in which I ever saw a regular good
seaman paralyzed by fear at the dangers of the sea.
Several of the sailors were seen on their knees at
prayer, but most were found ready to do their duty.*

When at last they could sail again, they headed
up the coast of Chile, which was then a Spanish
possession. Spain had received British help to get
rid of Napoléon. But now Chile was in revolt
against the mother country, so the Chilean port

of Valparaíso was safe and Porter anchored there for a few days.

After taking provisions, the *Essex* sailed up the Peruvian coast in search of British whalers. But unlike Chile, Peru was very much under Spanish control, and Spain sided with England in this conflict. Peruvian coast guard vessels sailed these waters and frequently took over American whalers on behalf of England. The *Essex* captured a Peruvian vessel, the *Nereyda*, with the crews of two American whalers it had taken on board. Renamed the *Essex Junior*, this vessel was used as an escort for the *Essex* as it headed for the Galápagos Islands. Among these islands, seven or eight British whaling ships were captured by the Americans. All told, there would be about fifteen "prizes" taken in this expedition.

Captain Porter decided to send some of the ships from the Galápagos to Valparaíso. On their way back, near Callao, the port of Lima, Peru, they recaptured the American ship *Alexander Barclay*, which had been taken by the Peruvians for the British. As a "prize vessel," it would now be under the command of a "prize crew" of Captain Porter's choosing. He selected Midshipman David Farragut to command the ship a distance of 2,500 miles, from Callao to Valparaíso! *This was an important event in my life*, wrote Farragut later, *and when it was decided that I was to take the ship to Valparaíso, I felt no little pride at finding myself in command at twelve years of age.*

Understandably, the captain of the *Barclay* was not in the mood to take orders from a mere boy. In his journal, Farragut described their confrontation:

When the day arrived for our separation from the squadron, the captain was furious, and very plainly intimated to me that I would "find myself off New Zealand" in the morning, to which I most decidedly demurred. We were lying still, while the other ships were fast disappearing from view, the commodore going North and the Essex Junior, *with her convoy, steering to the South for Valparaíso. I considered that my day of trial had arrived (for I was a little afraid of the old fellow, as every one else was). But the time had come for me at least to play the man; so I mustered up courage and informed the captain that I desired the maintopsail filled away, in order that we might close up with the* Essex Junior. *He replied that he would shoot any man who dared to touch a rope without his orders; he "would go his own course, and had no idea of trusting himself with a d---d nutshell"; and then he went below for his pistols. I called my right-hand man of the crew and told him my situation. I also informed him that I wanted the maintopsail filled. He answered with a clear "Ay, ay, sir!" in a manner which was not to be misunderstood, and my confidence was perfectly restored. From that moment I became master of the vessel, and immediately gave all necessary orders for making sail, notifying the captain not to come on deck with his pistols unless he*

*wished to go overboard, for I would really have had
very little trouble in having such an order obeyed.
I made my report to Captain Downes [of the* Essex
Junior], *on rejoining him; and the captain also told
his story, in which he endeavored to persuade
Downes that he only tried to frighten me. I replied
by requesting Captain Downes to ask him how he
succeeded; and to show him that I did not fear him,
I offered to go back and proceed with him to Valparaíso. He was informed that I was in command,
he being simply my adviser in navigating the vessel
in case of separation. So, this being understood, I
returned to the* Barclay, *and everything went on
amicably up to our arrival in Valparaíso.*

Word of the ravages of the *Essex* got to England.
The British sent a small squadron to get this lone
commerce-destroying ship. It consisted of the
sloops *Cherub* and *Raccoon,* and the frigate
Phoebe. Captain Porter heard from the American
consul in Buenos Aires that the British were coming after him. So the *Essex* and the *Essex Junior*
headed for the Marquesas Islands, far out in the
South Pacific, to refit and get provisions. There
were daily drills for the crews and when they
were ready for action, the ships headed back for
Valparaíso. This port was neutral and both British and American ships docked there.

The British ships *Phoebe* and *Cherub* approached four days after the return of the *Essex.*
The British knew that half the American crew was
ashore on liberty. The *Phoebe* ignored the fact

that they were in a neutral port and made straight
for the American ships, coming within fifteen feet
of the *Essex*. Captain Porter noticed that its captain was James Hillyar, an old friend of his from
years past, when both were on duty in the Mediterranean. Porter thought that Hillyar wanted to
greet him. The *Phoebe* became sandwiched between the *Essex* and the *Essex Junior*. The Americans returned to their ships and were ready
within fifteen minutes, aching to fight. But Porter
thought of the neutrality of the place. A young
American sailor was ready by the cannons, match
in hand, until a lieutenant stopped him. Captain
Hillyar, noticing how badly positioned he was,
changed his mind and didn't fire. The *Phoebe* was
allowed to move away, untouched, and drop an-
chor astern. "Had that gun been fired," Farragut
later said, "I am convinced that the *Phoebe* would
have been ours."

The enemy crews fraternized in the town for
several days; their captains sat down together,
too. Had he been in Porter's shoes, Hillyar told
Porter, he would have fired. Hillyar also said that
Porter would regret not firing into the *Phoebe*.

A few days later, the British ships began cruis-
ing outside of the mouth of Valparaíso's harbor.
The American ships were blockaded. At the end
of March, a fierce gust of wind broke the cable
moorings of the *Essex*. The little ship was thrown
into the harbor. Though still in neutral waters,
the British ships pursued the American vessel.
The *Essex* was outnumbered and outgunned. The

crew knew they could lose their lives, but "all were ready to die at their guns rather than surrender," Farragut recalled.

The fear of that day stayed with the young midshipman for a long time: "I well remember the feelings of awe produced in me by the approach of the hostile ships." But Farragut would not be paralyzed: "I performed the duties of captain's aid, quarter-gunner, powder-boy, and, in fact, did everything that was required of me. I generally assisted in working a gun, would run and bring powder from the boys, and send them back for more."

Fire broke out on board several times. The two-hour-long battle was fiery and bloody; of the 258 men of the *Essex*, 66 were wounded and 58 were killed. Captain Porter ordered the survivors to jump overboard to swim to safety. However, on noticing that the ship was sinking, he decided to surrender in order to save the wounded men. Farragut was ordered to throw overboard the signal book, the book where all the ship's records were kept. Then he joined the other midshipmen throwing the pistols and other small arms overboard so the enemy couldn't have them.

Among the prisoners taken by the *Phoebe* was Midshipman David Farragut. "I was so mortified at our capture that I could not refrain from tears," he said about that moment. But then, he was not yet thirteen years old, and had just lived through one of the worst episodes of his naval career.

Captain Porter reached an agreement with

Captain Hillyar and the Americans were paroled
and sent home on the *Essex Junior*, which had to
sail unarmed. They arrived in New York on July
7, 1814, and David Farragut returned quietly to
school in Chester, Pennsylvania. School life was
vastly different than his life at sea, but he adapted
himself promptly and well to the circumstances.
Recalling those days in later years, he said, "I do
not regret the time passed at this school, for it
has been of service to me all through life."

On December 24, 1814, the British and the
Americans formally ended their hostilities.

The next few years were busy but more peaceful
for David Farragut. In 1815 he went to sea for the
first time without Captain Porter. In 1816 he was
assigned to the first of several tours of duty cruis-
ing the Mediterranean. In Málaga, Spain, the
Spaniards treated Farragut as one of their own.
He was very much in demand to dance with many
highborn ladies and he acted as an interpreter
more than once.

Charles Folsom, the chaplain of the first ship
of the Mediterranean squadron, would become
Farragut's lifelong friend. Folsom instructed
young midshipmen in reading and writing, and
noticed that Farragut was bright and exceptionally interested in learning.

In the summer of 1817, Midshipman Farragut
heard that George Farragut had died in Louisiana. Though he had not lived with his father since
childhood, he was still greatly attached to him.

The chaplain was there for the grieving young man.

In the winter of that same year, Folsom was appointed the American consul to Tunis (present-day Tunisia), in the north of Africa. The navy and Captain Porter gave Folsom permission to take Farragut with him. Farragut soaked up learning and culture in that ancient land. Folsom tutored him for almost a year, and only sent him away when there was an outbreak of the plague. Folsom taught mathematics, English literature, French, and Italian, and on his own, Farragut learned Arabic. He just loved languages and communicating with different people.

In the fall of 1819, while stationed off Gibraltar, eighteen-year-old Midshipman Farragut was appointed acting lieutenant of the brig *Shark*. This was an important moment in his life. He felt mature in the company of men, not boys, and felt fortunate for having responsibility at an early age, "having observed, as a general rule, that persons who come into authority late in life shrink from responsibility, and often break down under its weight."

Farragut arrived in Norfolk, Virginia, in 1820. There he met and fell in love with a young woman named Susan C. Marchant, daughter of Jordan and Fanny Marchant, of Norfolk, but they couldn't marry as soon as they would have liked because he was assigned to duty in the Caribbean in 1822.

Captain Porter was the commander of this new expedition that had been dubbed the "Mosquito Fleet," because of the insect-ridden areas where they would be. Sailing under Porter meant a lot to Farragut, and it eased somewhat the unhappiness of leaving his fiancée. The fleet's assignment was to clear the West Indies of pirates, since they were burning and plundering American vessels on the Caribbean Sea. All around Cuba, Haiti, Santo Domingo, and Puerto Rico they chased the bandits, on the water and on land. One of their many casualties was the dreaded Diablito — "Little Devil." He and his band were aboard a schooner, in a cove, when the fleet barges *Gallinipper* and *Mosquito* found them. Diablito ordered his crew to fire, but they were unable to inflict much damage on the Americans. When they saw they couldn't win, the pirates jumped into the sea and made for the shore. Crewmen from one of the barges boarded the schooner without a struggle. As Diablito himself was about to escape, he was recognized by the Spanish pilot of the barge, who asked for and received permission to shoot the bandit.

A few days later, two fleet barges chased a schooner belonging to a pirate named Domingo. Though bloodthirsty like the others, he was said to be sort of a gentleman. One anecdote told of the time Domingo gave the Americans letters that the pirates had intercepted from their families. Domingo and his people were luckier than Diablito and his band — Domingo himself escaped with just a wound in one arm; only one of his men was killed, and no one was captured.

Pursuing pirates on land, by foot, Farragut and his party found some pirates' hiding places in Cuba — but they were vacant. Several large houses in the middle of the wilderness had been abandoned as the party approached. Numerous caves nearby could hide up to a thousand men. The caves, too, were unoccupied by people, but brimming with treasures and arms. The Americans burned the houses and took the booty to their ships. By coincidence, Farragut's older brother, Lieutenant William Farragut, was in the area. After thirteen years without seeing each other, the brothers had a reunion.

David Farragut and Susan Marchant were married upon his return to Norfolk in 1824. Captain Porter was in Washington, D.C., recovering from an attack of yellow fever. The newlyweds went to stay with him for a few weeks and then returned to Norfolk, where they started an austere and frugal life together. Farragut's monthly salary was only $25; it went up to $40 in 1825, with his promotion to lieutenant. From whatever he made, he sent money to his sisters, Nancy and Elizabeth, who were living with their respective foster families in New Orleans.

In the middle part of his life, Farragut became quite interested in recovering pieces of his family history. He was fascinated by a book of old Spanish poems in which the troubador Mossen Jaime Febrer praised the heroic deeds of his ancestor

Pedro Ferragut. He adopted as his own the horse-shoe design found on the coats of arms of all the old Ferraguts of Minorca.

From that period until the beginning of the Civil War, life consisted of routine duty for Farragut. When General Lafayette came to America for a visit, Farragut was on the *Brandywine*, the ship that took the visitor back home to France. He went to Argentina twice, where he met and befriended General Rosas, who would later become president and dictator of that South American country. He went to Brazil and paid his respects to the emperor, Dom Pedro I. He had shore duties in the United States.

People who served under Farragut said that he was greatly interested in them and their well being. They, in turn, loved him. One officer who served under him on the man-of-war *Natchez* said, "Never was the crew of a man-of-war better disciplined, or more contented and happy. The moment all hands were called and Farragut took the trumpet, every man under him was alive and eager for duty."

In 1838, with France and Mexico at war, Farragut commanded the sloop-of-war *Erie*, sailing to the coast of Mexico to safeguard American interests. He carefully watched the French bombardment of Veracruz from the sea and the valiant defense of the Mexicans. What he learned then would help him later on.

Farragut came back home to Norfolk in January 1839. His wife, Susan, had been frail for a good portion of their married life and suffered greatly with neuralgia, a painful nerve disease, and other ailments. He had tried to spend as much time as he could with her. Now she was crippled and declining rapidly, so he decided not to go to sea in order to care for her full time. His devotion to his wife won him the admiration of all of Norfolk.

Susan Farragut died in December 1840 and shortly thereafter her grieving husband requested sea duty. A new tour took him to Brazil and Argentina again. In 1841, while still in South America, he was promoted to commander.

At the end of 1843, David Farragut married Virginia Loyall, eldest daughter of William Loyall, one of the most distinguished and respected citizens of Norfolk. Their son, Loyall, was born in 1844. Loyall Farragut later wrote a biography of his father, *The Life of David Glasgow Farragut*, published in 1879. The book includes the elder Farragut's journals and letters.

The commander saw action in the Mexican War (1846–48) but his involvement was limited — a great disappointment to him — because the bulk of that operation fell to the army. At the end of that war, all the land from Texas to California became part of the United States. Farragut was stricken on his ship during a yellow fever outbreak. His doctor thought Farragut might die. Still very weak on his return to New Orleans, Farragut learned that his brother, William, was dying. Crippled with arthritis, William Farragut had retired from active duty years earlier. His deathbed wish was to see David, but it was not to be. When David Farragut arrived, it was time to attend his brother's funeral.

Farragut was constantly busy during the 1850s. In 1851–52 he was in Washington, D.C., working on a new regulations manual for the navy. In 1852–54, in Norfolk, he was assistant inspector of ordnance (military weapons). In 1854 he was assigned to create a navy yard at Mare Island, off San Francisco, California. He returned to the East Coast by way of the Isthmus of Panama, which he crossed on muleback because the Panama Canal had not been built yet.

In 1855, Farragut was made captain — after fifty years of service. It took him that long to reach the highest rank the navy had up to that time. He had joined the service much too young and there were many others ahead of him for promotions.

In 1860, two years after Abraham Lincoln stated, "This government cannot endure permanently half *slave* and half *free*," Farragut returned from a tour of duty in the Gulf of Mexico. One month later, Abraham Lincoln was elected president. The nation was facing great trials and tribulations, and Farragut's home state of Virginia was poised to secede.

The Southern states officially formed the Confederacy in February 1861. In April, Confederate soldiers attacked Fort Sumter, South Carolina. The Civil War had begun.

Farragut discussed the issues with his friends and colleagues many times and always expressed his opinions firmly. One day, while in a tavern in Norfolk, he said that it was wrong for Confederates to attack an army fort, and that it was right that President Lincoln had called for 75,000 volunteers to defend the Union. A man countered, in belligerent tones, that a person with such sentiments could not live in Norfolk, and the crowd shouted its approval. The captain knew what he had to do now. He replied with conviction, "Very well, I can live somewhere else."

Farragut hurried home and told his wife that he was in danger in Norfolk. He had seen it in the people's faces and heard it in their voices. He would leave, he said. She could choose to stay with her own relatives or follow him North. Without a moment's hesitation, Virginia Farragut chose to go with her husband. That evening, the Farraguts abandoned their Norfolk home and possessions for good. Eventually, their journey took them to New York. They settled in a small cottage in the village of Hastings, on the Hudson River. In his new Northern home, people thought he might be a spy and spread hideous rumors about him. They suspected the loyalty of a man who was a Southerner by birth, residence, and marriage.

However, Farragut knew exactly who he was and what he stood for. He hoped for sea duty, but when the assignment came, it was to a desk job in New York City. He was appointed a member

of a board that recommended officers for retirement from active duty. It was important work
but Farragut was a man of action.

As the Civil War raged, the South and the North
were trying out new technological advances. The
South was the first to try a strange ship that could
submerge (the submarine), and both sides tried
out ships covered with iron (the ironclads) that
sustained little damage when shelled.

By late 1861, the Union had recaptured some
of the forts it had lost earlier, but the entire area
between Memphis, Tennessee, and the Gulf of
Mexico was still controlled by the Confederates.
President Lincoln decided to take a bold, risky
plan of action. A fleet of wooden ships would bombard Fort Jackson and Fort St. Philip, the seaside
defenders of New Orleans, destroy the Confederate ships, and capture the city. Then the army
would come and maintain control. They dubbed
the plan "Anaconda," after the giant snake that
kills its prey by constriction. The most immediate
problem was deciding who would be in charge of
the fleet.

Captain David Dixon Porter, Farragut's foster
brother, was one of Lincoln's advisors, and he
said that Farragut was the person for the job. But
Farragut was from the South, Porter's colleagues
contended, and they weren't totally sure of the
loyalty of a Southerner. Besides, Farragut was
sixty years old and might lack the stamina for
the operation. Porter convinced them that Farragut was a loyal Union man and that his physical

condition was excellent, due in part to his daily exercise routine.

So in January 1862, David G. Farragut was appointed to the command of the Western Gulf Blockading Squadron. His flag was hoisted on the *Hartford*, a 22-gun sloop, 225 feet long and 44 feet wide, a vessel equipped with sails as well as steam power. Three similar ships, the *Brooklyn*, the *Richmond*, and the *Pensacola*, were also in the fleet that headed from Hampton Roads, Virginia, to the Gulf of Mexico and Louisiana. An assortment of other sloops, gunboats, and mortar schooners became part of the mighty fleet as well — all told, twenty-seven vessels carrying 200 guns and 700 men.

At long last, Farragut was flag officer of a large fleet. He was fully aware of what lay ahead and he was ready.

I have now attained what I have been looking for all my life — a flag — and having attained it, all that is necessary to complete the same is a victory, he wrote to his wife. *If I die in the attempt it will only be what every officer has to expect. He who dies in doing his duty to his country, and at peace with God, has played out the drama of life to the best advantage. The great men in our country must not only plan but execute. Success is the only thing listened to in this war, and I know that I must sink or swim by that rule. Any man who is prepared for defeat would be half defeated before he commenced.*

I hope for success; shall do all in my power to secure it, and trust to God for the rest.

The Confederate defenses were formidable. The mouth of the Mississippi, with its five channels, contained large deposits of mud; the larger ships could not sail through it, so they had to be dragged across. Twenty miles above the mouth were the two heavily prepared forts. Past that were the river flotilla and the Confederate fleet, and a hundred miles up the river was New Orleans, the queen of the Confederacy.

Farragut's opinion was that the forts should not be attacked first. He thought that the fleet could not defeat the forts at the beginning, but that the vessels should run past them and head directly toward the city. But he had to obey the Secretary of the Navy whose orders were to take the forts first. So, David Dixon Porter, who had been the architect of this part of the plan and was one of the commanders of the expedition, was put in charge of the shelling of the forts.

For six days the forts were shelled, but they never ceased returning the fire. One night, Farragut sent a couple of vessels up river to clear the fleet's path of obstacles. He had made up his mind to amend the plan and go to the city without subduing the forts first. It was a big gamble, and Porter objected, but Farragut was the flag officer in charge of the fleet.

The wooden hulls of the ships were crisscrossed with chain ropes and then covered with mud from the river. The ropes made the ships stronger; the mud made the ships hard to see from the shore at night. The decks were painted white so the crewmen could see better, in outline, what they needed. Trees were tied to the masts of the slower-moving boats so the forts would think the boats were trees from the other shore.

Under the cover of darkness the fleet headed towards New Orleans, with the smaller vessels in the lead. But they were soon discovered by the forts and the Confederate vessels. It was reported that the fire aimed from one side to the other made the night bright as day. The *Hartford* was set afire by a fire raft, but the flames were quickly extinguished. "It was the most anxious night of my life," said Farragut. "I felt as if the fate of my country and my own life and reputation were all on the wheel of fortune."

Fourteen Union vessels ran past the forts and only one was lost while they destroyed the Confederate flotilla. Union casualties were 37 killed, 149 wounded. For the Confederates, the toll was 73 killed, 73 wounded in the 10 ships that sank or burned; 11 killed, 37 wounded in the forts.

Through a defiant and menacing mob, two officers from the expedition walked valiantly to the New Orleans city hall for the surrender of the city on April 25. The two forts formally surrendered on April 28. Any help that could come to the Confederacy through the Gulf of Mexico was effectively cut off.

The Confederates had lost this battle but they

had not lost the war. Orders were for Farragut's
fleet to sail up the Mississippi River. The commander tried to convince the navy that the con-
ditions of the river were not appropriate for his
ships and that his supplies were not adequate.
The orders remained to "clear the river through,"
and Farragut agreed to advance upon Vicksburg,
Mississippi. "I hope for the best," he said, "and
pray God to protect our poor sailors from harm."

Farragut's fleet ran past the defenses at Vicksburg not once but several times and inflicted
much damage to one of the most precious vessels
of the Confederates, the ironclad ram *Arkansas*.
But the city could not be taken due to lack of
troops.

On August 12, 1862, Farragut, who had returned to New Orleans following orders, received
his commission as rear admiral of the United
States Navy. In July, Congress had enacted legislation to create that rank so it could be awarded
to Farragut for his brilliant success. About this
he wrote to his wife: *It is gratifying to me that my
promotion should not have rested simply on my
seniority, but that my countrymen were pleased to
think that it was fairly merited.*

In order to repair the vessels and obtain provisions, Farragut took his ships to Pensacola,
Florida, where they remained until the end of that
summer. There he learned that there was much
enemy activity again in Vicksburg, Mississippi,
and in Port Hudson, two hundred miles away

from that city. So back to the Mississippi River
the fleet sailed.

Between March and July 1863, the naval forces
under Farragut, in conjunction with land army
forces under General Ulysses S. Grant, fought
fiercely against Vicksburg and Port Hudson. At
one point the *Hartford* found itself isolated from
the rest of the fleet between both defensive sites.
"My last dash past Port Hudson was the best
thing I ever did," Farragut later said, "except
taking New Orleans. It assisted materially in the
fall of Vicksburg and Port Hudson." Both places
finally surrendered in August. Now the ships
could be kept focused upon Mobile, Alabama, the
next most important Confederate city after New
Orleans.

In August, Rear Admiral Farragut went home
to New York for much needed rest, and stayed
until January 1864. Then he returned to the Gulf
of Mexico to move against Mobile. He knew
the Confederates would be heavily prepared,
much more than immediately after the surrender of New Orleans two years before. He had
wanted to attack Mobile at that time. But the
orders came only now, and he knew it was a job
that had to be done if the Union was to win the
war.

The Confederates had driven a double line of
stakes and dropped a triple row of torpedoes
(mines) and submarine mortar-batteries to keep
Farragut from entering the bay. Some of the Con-

federate fighting ships were better and stronger than their Union counterparts. One of the best rebel ships was the *Tennessee*, a large ironclad ram, fast and powerful. The *Tennessee* was waiting in the bay along with three gunboats. The rebel fleet was tiny but strong. The admiral held back until four small ironclads, of a type called monitors, joined his twenty-one wooden vessels.

The fighting started early in the morning when the Union monitor *Tecumseh* fired two shots and attempted to cross the line of torpedoes, heading for the *Tennessee*. Suddenly the *Tecumseh* struck a torpedo and sank. Farragut's wooden ships were now a target of the rebel vessels and the guns of Fort Gaines and Fort Morgan, the guardians of Mobile. The Union officers hesitated. Rear Admiral Farragut asked, "What's the trouble?" He was told, "Torpedoes ahead!" Farragut responded with a line that would become famous: "Damn the torpedoes! Go ahead. Four bells [full speed]!"

The *Hartford*, his flagship, took the lead straight for the line of torpedoes. Farragut gambled because he thought that most of the torpedoes were poorly made and would not work. The speechless crew heard a scraping sound against the copper bottom of the ship but there was no explosion. The old strategist had been right! Farragut entered the bay and victory was practically assured. The other vessels of his fleet, many badly damaged from the attack from the fort and the enemy gunboats, followed. Most of the Union ships were anchored in the harbor a couple of hours later, when the *Tennessee* sailed into view, headed for the *Hartford*. One of Farragut's smaller ships, the *Monongahela*, went straight against the *Tennessee*. The valiant little ship split open as it crashed into the side of the ironclad while the ironclad remained unharmed. The *Hartford* and the rest of Farragut's fleet then shelled the *Tennessee*, until finally the rebel ironclad was beaten and it raised the white flag of surrender.

The Union fleet was badly damaged and 200 sailors had been killed. The Confederacy's dead were only 12 and the wounded, 20, but 243 of their men had been captured. "This was the most desperate battle I ever fought since the days of the *Essex*," said Farragut after it was over.

The exhaustion of the last six hard months, combined with his advanced age, began to show on David Farragut's strong body. He requested time to rest and sailed for New York in November, after having supervised the operation of clearing the Mobile area of torpedoes. He was welcomed as a hero. In December, the city of New York gave him a $50,000 check to buy a house. The same month, both houses of Congress created the rank of vice admiral of the United States Navy in order to award the new rank to Farragut. There were parties in his honor in New York and other cities. At first he thought party-going was more difficult than commanding a ship, but in time he came to enjoy his celebrity and the attention it brought him.

In November 1864, President Lincoln was re-
elected and on April 9, 1865, the Confederate
forces surrendered. A few days later, on April 14,
the president was shot; he died the next day.
There would be many changes in the reunited
country.

In 1866, another act of Congress created the
rank of admiral of the United States Navy, and
again, David G. Farragut was its first recipient.

In 1867, Admiral and Mrs. Farragut boarded
the steam frigate *Franklin*, heading his new
squadron for a special goodwill tour of Europe.
President Andrew Johnson and his cabinet attended the elegant party given on board before
sailing. During the next sixteen months, Farragut
was welcomed as a hero and treated as royalty
wherever he went — England, France, Belgium,
Holland, Denmark, Sweden, Russia, Italy, and
Greece. He was entertained by Queen Victoria
and the Duke of Edinburgh; Emperor Napoleon
III and Empress Eugénie; Grand Duke Constan-
tine; Pope Pius IX; and many others.

In Spain, Queen Isabel II told him, "I am glad
to welcome you to Spain . . . I am proud to know
that your paternal ancestors came from my do-
minions." The admiral renewed his acquaintance
with the Countess of Montijo, one of his dance
partners in Málaga nearly half a century earlier.
But the highlight and most endearing moment of
this tour still awaited him — a visit to Ciudadela,
capital of the island of Minorca, the birthplace of
Jorge Ferragut, his father. He was eager to learn

more about his ancestry firsthand.

The day of his arrival in Ciudadela, December 27, was declared a holiday. The admiral was given a copy of his father's baptismal record. A member of his traveling party wrote: *I am confident that, had there been an election that day for governor of the Balearic Islands, or for king of Spain itself, the admiral would have been chosen without opposition.* The celebrations lasted several days.

When Farragut returned home in 1868, all he wanted was rest. He was feeling wearier and weaker all the time, but his stature and fame would not permit repose. Some politicians approached him with the idea of launching his candidacy to be president of the United States. He declined, saying, "My entire life has been spent in the navy. By a steady perseverance and devotion to it I have been favored with success in my profession, and to risk that reputation by entering a new career at my advanced age, and that career one of which I have little or no knowledge, is more than anyone has a right to expect of me."

In September 1868, Queen Isabel II was deposed in Spain. The turmoil following that event prompted an article entitled "A Suggestion for the Spaniards" in the *Army and Navy Journal*, a publication from the United States. The suggestion was that the Spaniards should make David G. Farragut their king or emperor in order to solve the problem of succession to the Spanish throne. His qualifications were impeccable, the article stated — Spanish ancestry, knowledge of the language, naval experience, ties to the United States. There are no records of the admiral's reaction to the article, but it can be imagined.

Official duty of inspecting navy yards took the admiral to California in 1869. On his way back he survived a heart attack, but he never regained his full strength. In August 1870, sailing with his family to Portsmouth, New Hampshire, to visit an old navy friend, he became ill, but on hearing the guns fired in official salute, he dressed in full military uniform, went up on deck, and said, "It would be well if I died *now*, in harness." He had the feeling it wouldn't be long. A few days later he boarded an old sloop in the harbor. There he told an old sailor, "This is the last time I shall ever tread the deck of a man-of-war." And it was, for on August 14, 1870, Admiral Farragut, age sixty-nine, died quietly and peacefully at his friend's home. His fifty-eight years of service constitute another record unbroken to date.

Farragut's body was taken by ship from Portsmouth to New York City. The U.S. government planned a state funeral of a magnitude usually reserved for presidents. September 30, the day of the funeral, was declared a day of mourning, and all schools, banks, and businesses were closed. President Grant and his cabinet headed the funeral procession; 10,000 soldiers and sailors also attended. Burial was in Woodlawn Cemetery, in the Bronx, New York.

The United States government erected a statue of the admiral in the heart of Washington, D.C., and that area is called Farragut Square. In New York City a committee of citizens commissioned a statue, which was placed in Madison Square Park, where it still stands today.

David Glasgow Farragut is considered the greatest naval hero of his day. He was one of only twenty-nine individuals inducted into the Hall of Fame for Great Americans, in New York City, in 1900, the year the hall was established. The bust representing him, unveiled on May 5, 1927, was the gift of the Naval Order of the United States and a group of private citizens.

Honors have been bestowed upon Farragut in more recent times, too. In 1953, the Naval Academy at Annapolis received a plaque from Mahón, the city-port where the admiral's last European journey ended, commemorating that visit; and in 1970, a monument was dedicated to his memory in the land of his paternal ancestors.

2
Severo Ochoa

Severo Ochoa was a medical doctor who became a biochemist and received the highest and most prestigious of awards, the Nobel Prize, in 1959. From the very early years of his career, he worked with or was influenced by Nobel Prize winners. It was as if he had been born to win the award.

Severo Ochoa was named after his father, a lawyer and businessman, who lived with his wife, Carmen de Albornoz, in northern Spain. He was born in Luarca, province of Asturias, on September 24, 1905, the last of seven children. His father died when Severo was seven, and the family then moved to Málaga, in southern Spain.

Young Severo studied at an elementary school run by the Jesuits and at the public high school in the same city. Those who knew him then have said that in high school his interest in anatomy and physiology was quite remarkable.

Severo Ochoa then attended the University of Málaga and became interested in the writings of Dr. Santiago Ramón y Cajal. Ramón y Cajal was a professor at the University of Madrid. He was also a neurologist who had received the Nobel Prize for physiology or medicine in 1906, for his work on the nervous system.

In 1921, at age sixteen, Ochoa received a science degree in Málaga. The next year he enrolled at the University of Madrid to study medicine, but Ramón y Cajal had just retired when Ochoa arrived.

Ochoa was bitten by the research bug early on. He spent his summer vacation in 1927 at the University of Glasgow, Scotland, doing research in physiology. In 1929 he received his doctor of medicine degree, with honors, from the University of Madrid, and immediately traveled to Germany.

Germany was then the center of biochemical research. Dr. Ochoa worked at the Kaiser Wilhelm Institute for Physiology in Heidelberg from 1929 to 1931. His mentor there was Otto Meyerhof, a winner of the 1922 Nobel Prize in physiology or medicine for his work on the biochemistry of muscle. Meyerhof is considered one of the founders of modern biochemistry.

In Meyerhof's laboratory, Ochoa studied the sources of energy for contraction of the muscles. He found out certain aspects of the muscles' work that had not been previously known. In his book, *German-Jewish Pioneers in Science 1900–1933*,

David Nachmanson, another Meyerhof student, says:

Severo Ochoa was considered by Meyerhof to be his most brilliant pupil, as Meyerhof told the author [Nachmanson] on several occasions. He was deeply impressed by Ochoa's lucid and penetrating mind, by his rapid grasp of the essentials of a problem, by his personality, originality, and intuition. He predicted that Ochoa would become one of the truly great leaders of biochemistry of this generation because of his enthusiasm, his charisma, and his many leadership qualities.

Ochoa, in turn, said, "Meyerhof was the teacher who most contributed towards my formation, and the most influential in directing my life's work."

In 1931, Dr. Ochoa returned to Spain, married Carmen García Cobián, and was appointed to teach physiology and biochemistry at the University of Madrid. He was at the National Institute for Medical Research in London in 1932 doing research on the study of enzymes and their actions. His pioneering studies revealed the structure and mechanics of enzyme action. (Enzymes are substances that come from living cells, capable of producing chemical changes, such as digesting the food we eat.)

Dr. Ochoa returned to his post at the University of Madrid and was appointed chief of the physiology division at that school's Institute for Med-

ical Research in 1935. But the following year, the
Spanish Civil War erupted and any possibility of
doing scientific research in Spain was gone. Carmen and Severo Ochoa decided to leave the country, which was fortunate because the area where
the labs were located soon became a bloody bat-
tlefield. The Ochoas went to Germany, and Dr.
Ochoa returned to Meyerhof's laboratory.

In 1937, Dr. Ochoa went to do research at the
Marine Biological Laboratory at Plymouth, England. There he continued with his studies of enzymes. At one point his wife worked as his
collaborator. From Plymouth, Dr. Ochoa went to
the biochemical laboratory of Oxford University.
There he discovered some of the biochemical
properties and functions of vitamin B_1 (thiamine)
and biotin.

By 1941, the effects of World War II in England
made it very difficult for scientists to work in that
country. Dr. Ochoa then decided to accept the
invitation of Drs. Carl and Gerty Cori to work
with them at Washington University in St. Louis,
Missouri. The Coris headed a laboratory that at
the time was as famous as Meyerhof's laboratory
had been. This husband and wife team who
shared the Nobel Prize in physiology or medicine
in 1947 became Ochoa's last "formal teachers."

The following year, Dr. Severo Ochoa found a
long-term professional home at New York University College of Medicine, in New York City.
Meyerhof had also left Germany and was now in
Philadelphia. Ochoa, several other former stu-

dents, and their families remained very close friends with Meyerhof and his wife.

The Ochoas felt at home in New York City partly because of its cultural life. Carmen and Severo loved the opera and classical music, as well as museums and art. They found all of that in a city that is considered the capital of the arts in the United States. In addition to his work, Dr. Ochoa enjoyed color photography. He and Mrs. Ochoa, who never had children, traveled extensively throughout the world and delighted in visiting monuments and architectural masterpieces.

Dr. Ochoa's first appointment at NYU was as a research fellow. In 1945, he was appointed associate professor of biochemistry, and in 1946, professor of pharmacology, which is the science of drugs, their preparation, and effects. In 1946, he also took his first postdoctoral student, Dr. Arthur Kornberg. Later on, the names of Ochoa and Kornberg would be forever associated with each other.

In 1949, Dr. Ochoa spent a year as a visiting professor of biochemistry at the University of California at Berkeley before returning to NYU. "The delays in Ochoa's academic promotion were, to some measure, due to his own indifference," according to Francisco Grande and Carlos Asensio, students and colleagues of Ochoa. When offered promotions, Dr. Ochoa said, "Why do I need a professorship? I can do my work where I am now; will the research work not suffer if I become a department chairman?" It seems that what fi-

nally made him change his mind was the offer of
a well-equipped laboratory with the latest and
most up-to-date scientific equipment. That was
the lab of the chairman. Thus, Dr. Ochoa became
professor and chairman of the Department of Biochemistry in 1954, and two years later he and his
wife became U.S. citizens.

In October 1959, Dr. Ochoa received the greatest honor of his life. The Swedish Academy of
Sciences announced that the Nobel Prize in physiology or medicine had been awarded that year
to two doctors, Dr. Severo Ochoa, of New York
University College of Medicine, and Dr. Arthur
Kornberg, of Stanford University School of Medicine.

The Nobel Prize, established by Alfred B. Nobel, the Swedish inventor of dynamite and other
explosives, is awarded in various fields, including
science, economics, literature, and promoting
peace. For the science awards, Nobel's will states
that they are to be given for "major" discoveries.
The winners are selected among candidates from
all over the world. Ochoa was honored for the
test-tube synthesis of RNA; Kornberg, Ochoa's
one-time pupil, for the test-tube synthesis of
DNA.

DNA (deoxyribonucleic acid) is an extremely
large molecule that carries genetic information
and is present in the chromosomes of all cells.
RNA (ribonucleic acid) is the sister molecule of
DNA and acts as a sort of translator or messenger
for DNA. It uses the information in DNA to syn-

thesize protein and can even carry information from one cell to another.

Synthesis is what takes place when simpler compounds are combined to form more complex substances. It happens naturally. The "synthesis" of RNA and DNA in a test tube in a lab is almost like making a copy of living matter. Knowledge acquired in this manner can be extremely useful to the understanding of many things, such as trying to figure out why some cells become tumors and why some remain healthy. If this *why* is answered, it may be possible to find out *how* to cure certain diseases.

The two discoveries happened independently of each other. Ochoa came upon his discovery in 1955, almost accidentally, while doing research on plant and animal metabolism, the process taking place in the body that involves the distribution of nutrients and results in growth, energy production, elimination of wastes, and other body functions.

Kornberg says that he set out to find an answer. *But I had veered in that direction after my training in Ochoa's laboratory in 1946, and so perhaps in some sense the two discoveries were not unrelated at all*, writes Kornberg in his book, *For the Love of Enzymes*.

Naturally, Ochoa did not stop experimenting in his lab because he had won a Nobel Prize. He continued working at NYU until he retired, in 1974, making other important contributions to science. In 1975, he began his association with the Roche Biomedical Laboratories in Nutley, New Jersey.

Throughout the years, Dr. Severo Ochoa found hundreds of occasions to leave his lab and make presentations in conferences around the world. Up until his retirement from NYU, he had also written and published 246 scientific articles and two books, *The Genetic Key, Heredity's Chemical Base*, in 1964, and *Macromolecules: Biosynthesis and Function*, in 1970. After his retirement, he published another book, *Viruses, Oncogenes, and Cancer*, in 1985.

Starting with Alpha Omega Alpha, the honorary medical society, the list of Dr. Ochoa's memberships would fill pages. He belonged to scientific academies and societies in several South American and North American countries, most of western and eastern Europe, the former Soviet Union, and Israel. He received dozens of honors and awards from universities and institutions around the globe.

All the honors and awards meant a great deal to Ochoa, but one honor that must have meant more than most to him was his seventieth birthday party. In September 1975, the Spanish government organized a series of conferences and other activities in Madrid and Barcelona. Many of his colleagues from all over the world took part, among them ten biochemists who had also received the Nobel Prize. They all went to pay tribute to Ochoa for his inspiring leadership, his great contributions to science, and for the important part he played in the development of biochemistry.

Ochoa's one-time student and Nobel Prize co-winner, Kornberg, with B. L. Horecker, L. Cornudella, and J. Oró, collected all the presentations. They edited them and put them in a book, *Reflections on Biochemistry in Honour of Severo Ochoa*, which was published the following year. The famous painter Salvador Dalí made a painting for the book's cover. All of Ochoa's articles appearing in magazines and journals all over the world were collected in three volumes, each of them about 1,000 pages thick.

The "Institute of Molecular Biology Severo Ochoa" was inaugurated at this time. Juan Carlos and Sofía, who were then prince and princess and are now king and queen of Spain, were there for the celebrations.

After his magnificent party, Dr. Severo Ochoa returned to his lab in New Jersey. He died eighteen years later on November 1, 1993, of pneumonia in Madrid. His life's work is proof that science has no national borders, no language barriers.

3
Jaime Escalante

On December 31, 1930, high up in the Andes mountains, in La Paz, Bolivia's capital, Sara Gutiérrez de Escalante gave birth to her second child. The boy was given the name Jaime Alfonso Escalante Gutiérrez. Sara and her husband, Zenobio Escalante, already had a daughter. Later on, they would have another daughter and two sons.

Both Mr. and Mrs. Escalante were schoolteachers. At that time in Bolivia, public schoolteachers could not choose where they wanted to work when they first started but were sent where they were needed most. The greatest need was often in poor villages in the high plateau, known as *altiplano*, where the Aymará and the Quechua Indians live. Sara and Zenobio Escalante were assigned to one of those villages, Achacachi, not too far from Lake Titicaca, the highest lake in the world.

From very early on, Jaime showed he was a gifted child with a quick mind and great manual skills. It is said that he spent hours out-of-doors devising and building his own games. He was also fond of long walks through the town with his maternal grandfather, at which times grandpa and grandchild played word games.

Zenobio Escalante became an alcoholic. He behaved strangely and at times beat his wife and even his oldest son. When Jaime was nine, Sara de Escalante took her children, boarded a bus, and went to La Paz. With meager financial resources, their home in La Paz was in a small ground-floor apartment, which often flooded when it rained.

His first day at school, Jaime Escalante was attired in the same kind of clothes usually worn by Indian children on the *altiplano*. The city kids laughed when they saw him. But soon they would come to admire and respect him because he was better than everyone at arithmetic. He was also impressive in basketball, soccer, and handball. Handball was a game all children could play, even the poor. In Jaime's neighborhood there was a handball court, where he was often found.

Handball often got young Jaime in trouble with his mother. Sent for small purchases, he would bet the money at the handball court. However, the boy always managed to talk his older sister into lending him the money to cover the money he lost.

Jaime became a tough street kid and could have easily become a juvenile delinquent. But he was also interested in experiments of all kinds. His sisters recall that in his search for answers he often involved them in some of his experiments.

Zenobio Escalante showed up at his family's home in La Paz now and then. The children, especially the older ones, were unhappy when he came because he was often abusive to them. The children were generally happy with their mother and without their father.

When things improved a little financially, Sara de Escalante and her children moved to a slightly better house on a hillside. Some neighbors raised sheep and cows and others grew corn and barley in the vicinity.

At school, Jaime Escalante became known not only because he was smart, but also for his love of jokes and fistfights. Schoolwork in general bored him, with the exception of science and math. In those two subjects he excelled.

Sara de Escalante skimped enough to be able to send fourteen-year-old Jaime to a prestigious high school, San Calixto, run by Jesuit priests. Jaime Escalante liked San Calixto very much. The school had an atmosphere that made the students want to learn. In addition, the buildings and surroundings were beautiful.

The change in schools changed Jaime Escalante in some ways but not in others. He still engaged

in fistfights, but he also had a group of friends who got together for study sessions. They would go to the house of one of the boys at nine in the morning on a Saturday and study until seven at night. It was in those days that Escalante met Roberto Cordero, who became a lifelong friend.

Sara de Escalante was happy that her son was gifted, but his wild ways made her uneasy. She would lecture him about comments on his report card like "Jaime talks too much" or "Jaime likes his jokes."

Jaime would sometimes read a textbook ahead of the lesson his class was studying. When he finished all the problems, he'd borrow more advanced books, like his sister's chemistry books. He even took a physics book from a friend's house when he was told he could not borrow it.

A new physics teacher, French-born Father Descottes, came to San Calixto when Jaime was in the tenth grade. *The man was thin and gray and sarcastic*, an Escalante biographer has written, *but he made magic in a laboratory with an electric motor, a set of premeasured weights, a compass, and a small pendulum. Jaime volunteered to keep the laboratory clean if he could learn more about the instruments, and borrow some of the priest's books.*

Another favorite physics teacher later on was a man from Chile named Lincoyan Portus. Portus used to start his class with a story and then ask a student to repeat it. Escalante would always repeat the story and improve on it. This teacher also gave the students short unannounced quizzes, whenever he felt like giving them.

Jaime Escalante made good grades but he found a thousand ways to get in trouble at school so he was on the verge of being expelled many times. On the streets, he befriended all sorts of people and, by his own account, he learned something from everyone.

Jaime Escalante learned enough from a lot of sources to build his own room — walls, roof, windows, and all — an addition to his mother's house. When he was in his room, he buried himself in his books and dreamed of becoming an engineer.

Money for engineering school, however, was not available. Jaime Escalante had to take odd jobs after finishing high school and tried to figure out what to do with his life. One day his friend Roberto Cordero told him the admissions test for the Normal Superior, the teacher's college, would soon be given. "You always like to work with physics and math and chemistry," Cordero said. Escalante said no, he wasn't interested in teaching.

"If you don't like it, you can always change," Cordero said. "I'm going to take the exam. I want to be a chemistry teacher." So, with his friend going, Escalante said, "Can't hurt to give it a shot," and he also went for the exam. Both passed the test and started classes at the Normal Superior. Escalante soon became well known in the school for his colorful personality.

When Escalante was a sophomore, he got a lucky break. His old teacher Humberto Bilbao was working at the Ministry of Education and was in charge of teacher recruitment. A physics teacher at the American Institute had just died and a temporary replacement was needed. Bilbao asked several students in the upper classes to take the job but, for various reasons, they couldn't do it. They suggested Escalante. After all, Escalante considered himself an "Einstein."

Bilbao remembered the mischievous little boy whose mind was full of questions and ideas, and he asked the young man if he could teach. "I can teach anything you want me to," Escalante replied. So they went to the American Institute and the young man got his first teaching assignment. For the first time, Escalante saw boys and girls together in the same class. The custom in Bolivia was to have separate boys' schools and girls' schools. But the American Institute was run privately by American Methodist missionaries and things were different there.

Escalante had not yet taken any of the education classes that teachers are required to take in college. The principal was concerned about his lack of formal training, and with good reason, for Escalante's teaching technique left a lot to be desired.

But little by little, Escalante's technique improved. He spent hours and hours preparing to teach his class. However, he assigned the students so much material that when he gave them a short quiz many of them failed. He was crushed. He asked them to stay after school twice a week so they would be ready for the final exam.

In Bolivia, the same final exam was given to all the children in the same grade throughout the country. The teacher who taught the class did not prepare the test. The test was written and given by the Ministry of Education office. Escalante's students did very well on the final exam.

Escalante continued taking classes in his teacher's college. When his temporary job at the American Institute ended, Bilbao found another part-time job for him, as a physics teacher. It was at the Nacional Bolívar, a very good public school. Escalante said he had not taken all the courses on how to teach yet, he was only a junior. His old teacher told him it didn't matter, that Escalante could do it.

The principal of Nacional Bolívar said he liked the way Escalante prepared himself and his lesson plan, as well as the clear and loud way he spoke. But he suggested that the new teacher visit the class of an old science teacher to see how the experienced man conducted his class.

Escalante was fascinated by the old science teacher who paced the floor holding an animal's leg bone in his hand. The teacher constantly addressed the students and requested their participation. Afterwards, the veteran teacher told his new colleague, "A teacher has to be up on every trick, Jaime. That's the only way to get the good results. Anything you produce, anything that works, stop and analyze it. If it works, use it. Save it. Study it . . . Anything to get them [the students] to class." Escalante followed his advice and his teaching methods improved.

By his early twenties, Escalante still had not completed all the courses needed for graduation from the Normal Superior, but he was making money teaching. He was also dating two girls at the same time and partying frequently. His friend Roberto Cordero had married by then and his wife, Blanca, thought that Escalante should straighten out. She introduced Jaime Escalante to Fabiola Tapia.

Fabiola Tapia was a beautiful girl, very serious and proper. She was the eldest daughter of a family of evangelical Protestants who had lost a potato farm after one of the frequent revolutions in Bolivia. Her father had a degree from a small Bible college in California and worked as a schoolteacher in Torotoro, a small town in the *altiplano*. No alcohol was ever served in the Tapia home.

Knowing she had to support herself, Fabiola Tapia got a scholarship to attend high school in La Paz. Afterwards, she enrolled at the Normal Superior to become a teacher.

Courting the young woman, Jaime Escalante returned to the Normal Superior on a regular basis, not on and off as he had done since he started teaching. He was always there at break time to buy her snacks. He helped her and her friends with their math lessons. He made himself as charming and indispensable as possible. She thought he was quite special.

One day a fellow student who was teaching at San Calixto called Escalante and told him there was an opening for a physics teacher at his old high school. Escalante said he still lacked his teaching credential, but he was told it didn't matter because San Calixto was a private school.

At twenty-three, Jaime Escalante finally finished all his requirements and graduated from the Normal Superior. By then, he was already teaching at San Calixto, one of the best high schools in La Paz. He loved teaching almost as much as he loved Fabiola Tapia. At one point he was teaching in three different schools at the same time — his regular day job, an afternoon job, and an evening job. He was also tutoring privately, and he was so popular as a tutor that he had to send some students to his friend Roberto Cordero.

At San Calixto, Escalante became a legend. Students feared and loved him. He would give 50 to 100 problems a night for homework, but he would work with any pupil after school until there were no mistakes. He prepared students as a team and had them enter a major science and math contest. The first year they entered, his team placed second. The next year and all the following years, they always came in first.

The Tapia family was not too happy about Fabiola's romance with a Roman Catholic, but Escalante managed to win them over. Fabiola Tapia

and Jaime Escalante married in November 1954.
They went to live in a small house half a block
away from his mother. A year later, Jaime, Jr.,
also known as Jaimito, was born.

Alcohol was not allowed at home by Fabiola,
but Escalante kept on partying elsewhere. He
would go on his social rounds alone. This made
his wife unhappy and they often fought. He'd
promised to do better but would soon forget. Sara
de Escalante threatened her son, telling him she
would ask Fabiola's parents to take their daughter back home.

Life was a series of ups and downs for Fabiola
and Jaime Escalante. She began to think that
going to the United States would solve many of
their problems. Her brothers were going to study
in California, like their father, so they would have
relatives there.

Jaime Escalante did so well with his many jobs
that by 1961 they had a new comfortable home
and a car. They also had a chauffeur who took
Jaimito to school. When the car was not needed
by the family, the chauffeur was allowed to use
it as a taxi. Jaime was happy but Fabiola was
not. She disliked his drinking and partying the
most, and often talked about moving to the
United States.

Then something happened. Jaime Escalante
was invited to spend a year in Puerto Rico in a
special program of the Alliance for Progress, the
organization just started by the Kennedy administration. The participants were industrial arts

and science teachers from different Latin American countries.

During their stay in Puerto Rico, the U.S. State Department took the teachers to Pittsburgh, Pennsylvania, for an international conference on education. After the conference, they visited a high school in Tennessee, where Escalante was impressed by a physics lab in the school. He wondered how it would feel to teach in such a wonderful place.

When he returned to Bolivia and his wife again mentioned moving to California, Jaime Escalante said, "If we have any chance to go, we will go." That's all she needed to hear. A few months later, Fabiola had taken care of all the necessary papers. Her brother, Samuel Tapia, would be their official sponsor. Jaime, Sr., would go first in order to find a job and a place to live. After selling everything they owned, Fabiola and Jaime, Jr., went to live with her parents. She and the boy would wait there until Jaime, Sr., sent for them.

Jaime Escalante could not bear to say goodbye to his mother in person. Instead, he left a good-bye note.

Two days after boarding a plane in La Paz, Jaime Escalante arrived at Los Angeles International Airport, on Christmas Eve, 1963. His plane had made stops in half a dozen cities in South, Central, and North America. He was exhausted, confused, and uncharacteristically silent when his brother-in-law, Sam Tapia, met him.

Sam Tapia lived in Pasadena, near Los Angeles.

At night, he took courses at Pasadena City College; daytime, he had a job in the machine shop of a map-making company in Los Angeles. His younger brother, David, a student at Pasadena High School, lived with him. Jaime Escalante settled in with them. The first things he asked Sam were whether he could get any Bolivian food and about the job market.

Jobs were scarce in those days, especially for somebody like Jaime Escalante, who knew very little English. Sam Tapia took his brother-in-law to some car washes and restaurants but there was no job available.

Escalante memorized some English phrases and kept looking on his own. He finally found a job cleaning up in Van den Kamp's Restaurant, near Pasadena City College. He did his job very well and the boss was quite pleased.

Sam Tapia could not understand why his brother-in-law would want to stay in the restaurant business, given his previous interest in education. He finally talked Escalante into taking night courses at Pomona City College.

In order to enter the school, a student had to take an entrance examination. He or she could choose among many subjects for the test. Escalante chose math since it required less English. The instructor gave him a booklet and said the test would take two hours. Escalante finished the test in twenty-five minutes, with a perfect score. And so, Jaime Escalante enrolled in school again.

By May 1964, Escalante had been promoted to

head cook at Van den Kamp's. He changed the menu and the schedules. His boss talked of turning the whole business over to him.

The day Fabiola and Jaimito arrived in Los Angeles, Escalante could not go to meet them at the airport because he was too busy at work and there was no one to cover for him. Neither the job at Van den Kamp's nor smoggy Pasadena had crossed Fabiola's mind when she thought about living in the United States. It was true that her husband was making more money than he had been making in Bolivia, but he was an educated man and this was a blue-collar job. However, Jaimito was happy being with his dad again. Also, her husband had no time to go drinking with friends, and that was something she liked.

Whenever his wife brought up the subject of getting a better job, Escalante would tell her that being a cook was a temporary situation, until he learned English at the college. He'd say that one day he was going to send his credentials to get a good teaching job.

The California Department of Education sent a short form letter to Escalante in August. The letter said that the credentials he had sent were not good enough for teaching in California. He would have to take the American education curriculum before he could be considered for a teaching job. Escalante was bitterly disappointed. It would take him too long to get another teaching degree. He considered going back to Bolivia.

His wife told him that he didn't have to go back

to teaching: "You can go into electronics instead. You've always been interested in that. Isn't that one reason why we came to America? So you could do something different, perhaps work for NASA?"

When he calmed down, Jaime Escalante decided that his family would stay in the United States. His son was adjusting well and would have educational opportunities not available in Bolivia. The boy could study anything he wanted in this country, where it was like "a supermarket" of educational opportunities.

Fabiola Escalante got a job on the assembly line at the Burroughs Corporation plant in Pasadena. She was sure her husband could get a job there if he really wanted to. Burroughs was an electronics company and, in her opinion, Jaime was better qualified than many of the technicians who worked there. She started her campaign to get him to apply. When Jaime Escalante finally took the test at Burroughs, he scored one hundred percent. He was offered a job in the parts department, which he accepted.

In 1969, their second son, Fernando, was born and his mother left her assembly line job. Jaime Escalante kept working and advancing at the plant. By 1972, he was offered a supervisor's job at a new Burroughs plant in Guadalajara, Mexico, but he turned it down. Jaime Escalante would soon finish work for a bachelor's degree at Cal State. With a scholarship from the National

Science Foundation, Escalante got his teaching credentials at Cal State in 1973.

In 1974, Jaime Escalante had every credential needed to teach in California and applied to the Los Angeles Unified School District. He was asked where he wanted to teach. "A school," he said, not understanding at first that they were asking what type of ethnic community he wanted to deal with. He chose the Chicano community, East Los Angeles. For one thing, the students would be familiar with the Spanish language, for another, it was closer to his home in Monrovia. Jaime Escalante was unaware that in East Los Angeles gangs, poverty — and very bad schools — were abundant.

Escalante was offered three schools to choose from: Belvedere, a junior high school, and Roosevelt and Garfield, both senior high schools. Before making a decision, he was going to visit all three. He stopped at Garfield first. The principal told Escalante the school was getting a new computer lab and he would make him the computer teacher. That was it; he decided he'd teach at Garfield. There was no need to visit the other schools, so he canceled his other appointments.

On his first day at Garfield in September 1974, Escalante was handed his schedule: five math classes, no computer class. They had not been able to get the computer program in place. Then he went to a meeting with the other math teachers. One of them wanted to introduce a math program based on games and exercises to get teenagers interested. Escalante examined a textbook that was much too simple for high school students, as far as he was concerned. He thought of going back to his old job in electronics.

The day classes started was no better. The dress, the manner, the language of those students was completely inappropriate for school. Escalante had no room of his own and had to move from one place to another to teach his class. He soon became so discouraged that he told the principal he'd leave by the end of the school year.

The principal gave him a room that was in a state of disrepair. Escalante decided to get the students interested in helping him fix up the room. On a Saturday they all painted the walls, scrubbed the graffiti off the desks, and decorated the room with colorful posters.

Escalante continued his work of winning the students over. He played handball with them. ("If you beat me, you get an A. If you don't beat me, you do this homework.") Escalante never lost. He challenged the students every possible way, he teased them, he made them mad, he got them interested, he treated them as no one had ever treated them before.

Escalante insisted on absolute discipline, punctuality, and responsibility. One minute he was a harsh taskmaster, the next, a loving uncle who gave them hugs and candy. If he had to, he went to a student's home to talk to his or her parents, or phoned the parents . . . as early as seven in the morning. The students nicknamed Escalante "Kimo Sabe," what the Lone Ranger was called by his companion, Tonto. To this day, students still call him that, or "Kimo" for short.

Escalante's work and battles went on for several years and they included his colleagues and the administration as well. He had to fight for better textbooks, and for courses that challenged the students. Escalante contended that many of his colleagues thought the students didn't need tough courses because they were poor Hispanics who would not go to college. Jaime Escalante would not accept that point of view under any circumstances. He would prove to the world that among poor Hispanics there are as many people capable of going to college as among any other ethnic group.

Other teachers began to see that many of the things Escalante was saying were possible. A young math teacher, Ben Jiménez, coordinated classes with Escalante. Eventually, there were more regular math and algebra classes than remedial math classes at Garfield. Then, calculus classes were started, and after that, Advanced Placement calculus. High school students who take an Advanced Placement test and pass it can get one year's college credit for that subject. At Garfield, a good number took AP tests in languages and a handful of others took them in other subjects, but not in calculus.

By 1982, Escalante had prepared eighteen students to take the AP calculus test. They were all people who'd been up against incredible odds: one was a gang member; one could not study at night because the light bothered other members of her family who were sleeping; someone else had to work to help his family; the father of one student didn't want her to take the exam because she was a girl. There were eighteen different stories of hardships to overcome.

All eighteen students passed the test, but the Educational Testing Service, the office that gives the tests, accused fourteen of cheating.

Officials at ETS were not able to prove the students had cheated, but they said that the fourteen students had made the exact same mistake on one question. The students were notified at home during the summer that their scores would not stand, that they should take the test over.

The situation became a national scandal. People at Garfield High and other places said that ETS was racially biased because the students came from a poor Hispanic neighborhood. If the students had come from affluent neighborhoods, no cheating accusation would have been made, they argued.

For his part, Escalante said that if the students had made the same mistake it was because they had the same teacher. He wanted to talk to ETS officials but they would not discuss things with him or anyone else from the school.

ETS denied the racial charges and said that the students should retake the test in order to make sure they knew the subject. The whole summer was spent arguing about the situation. Some people at Garfield wanted the students to retake it, some did not. Some said that if they retook it, they would admit guilt; while others said that if they retook it, there would be absolutely no doubt.

The students themselves were confused, angry, and frustrated. They didn't know what to do. Escalante and Henry Gradillas, Garfield's principal, thought that the students should retake the test, but the students themselves were the ones who decided. Two of the students had moved away and chose not to take the test over, the other twelve chose to take it.

All twelve passed the AP calculus test the second time around — a test they said was more difficult than the first. Their teacher received hundreds of invitations to appear in conferences throughout the country, to lecture, and to give seminars. He was interviewed by newspapers, magazines, radio and TV stations.

The movie *Stand and Deliver* retold that incident at Garfield High School in Los Angeles. For his stirring performance as Escalante, actor Edward James Olmos was nominated for a 1988 Academy Award.

Jay Mathews, a newspaper reporter, decided to write a book about the incident but he did more than that — he wrote a complete biography of Jaime Escalante. It took Mathews five years to write that book, *Escalante: The Best Teacher in America*. By coincidence, it was published the year the movie was released but the projects were totally independent of each other.

Jaime Escalante continued teaching and preparing students to take the AP calculus test at Garfield. Every year the number of students taking it increased. At least as many girls as boys took it, sometimes, more girls than boys, disproving the theory that girls are less capable than boys in math.

In 1990, the Foundation for Advancements in Science and Education produced a TV series on math, science, and careers for grades 7–12. Called *Futures*[1] *with Jaime Escalante*, it consists of thirteen episodes, 12–15 minutes each. In each episode, Escalante shows how math is applied in the real world. Students get to see that math is relevant, and fun.

The series won a Peabody Award, a prestigious prize for educational materials. And it was so popular that the same team put together a second series in 1992, *Futures*[2] *with Jaime Escalante*.

The fact that Escalante was now a media star made other teachers at Garfield uncomfortable. Some said there were other teachers in the school doing wonderful work and they were not recognized. Some said Escalante did not share his methods and techniques with other colleagues, and that he paid no attention to school paperwork.

Be that as it may, Jaime Escalante decided he did not want to stay at Garfield. He certainly could pursue careers other than teaching. But teaching is in Escalante's blood. He moved to Hiram Johnson High School in Sacramento for the 1991–92 school year. Newspapers reported a drop in math achievement at Garfield after Escalante left, just as some had predicted would happen.

Hiram Johnson High School is different from Garfield in that it's not in an area as poverty-ridden as East Los Angeles. Also, the population includes Asians, Hispanics, Blacks, and Anglos. Students, however, need to produce more at this school, too, and Escalante is prepared to help them do just that. His classroom is as colorful as it was in Los Angeles, decorated with posters, mathematical equations, sayings, and advice all around. Games still abound. Students still come by and tell him, "Kimo, I'll see you tomorrow at seven A.M."

What does Jaime Escalante say of himself? He says that the person who most influenced him was his mother: "She was my mentor, the one who enlightened and motivated me."

He likes his profession because "children are the future of the country." He likes to tell parents to "make your son or daughter, as a child, see in you a sustaining force; as a teenager, a guiding intelligence; as a young person, a friend who gives advice."

To the students, Jaime Escalante likes to say that "knowledge is power" and that "school is the place that makes it possible for dreams to come true, the place where personality is shaped." The students, however, have to have *"ganas,"* that is, the desire to achieve their dreams.

What do students think of Jaime Escalante? When Angela Fajardo, formerly of Garfield High School, was an engineering student at Loyola Marymount, she wrote:

I hope more teachers follow the example of Mr. Escalante. He brought in props [toys, for example] to help us visualize and showed us that math was more than numbers. Instead of just concentrating on theory, he showed how the knowledge can be applied.

He convinced us that we were capable of doing any kind of math — that we could accomplish anything. By believing in us, he gave students confidence.

It seems clear, then, that Jaime Escalante's greatest contribution is to make students believe they can do it — whatever their goals may be. Escalante's unusual methods combined with his forceful personality have made him a great success.

4
Roberto Clemente

Gone but not forgotten. That's a headline likely to appear every year in at least one newspaper or magazine, usually on or before December 31. Every December 31, since 1972, Vera Clemente, her family, and friends go to a sad reunion on a beach in San Juan, Puerto Rico. The headline and the beach visit refer to Roberto Clemente, who was and is still called, "the pride of Puerto Rico." He died in a plane crash on December 31, 1972, within view of the beach, shortly after the plane took off on its way to a mission of mercy.

In the Spanish-speaking countries where baseball is popular — in the Caribbean, and Central and South America — Roberto Clemente is also remembered. In Nicaragua, people are likely to refer to him as "the unforgettable one." Clemente was not the first Hispanic baseball player in the

United States — there was one on the very first professional baseball team — and, as everyone knows, he was not the last.

Roberto Clemente, however, captured people's imaginations more than anyone else, not only as a great baseball player but as a very special human being, a living legend in his time.

Luisa Walker, the wife of Melchor Clemente, gave birth to a boy on August 18, 1934. Named Roberto, he was the youngest of five Clemente boys. The family also included a boy and a girl from Mrs. Clemente's previous marriage. They lived in San Antón, a poor neighborhood in Carolina, Puerto Rico. His sister once called Roberto "Momen" — a word with no particular meaning — and the nickname stuck. That's what he was often called by family and friends.

Roberto's parents were deeply religious and hard-working people who taught their children to be respectful, loving, and understanding. "Hate did not exist in my home," Roberto Clemente told a friend years later. "I never heard a dirty word at home. I never heard my mother or my father raise their voices."

The 1930s were very difficult years in Puerto Rico as well as in the mainland United States, but for the Clementes things weren't as bad as for other people. Mr. Clemente was a foreman in a sugar cane plantation, and therefore made more money than the regular workers. It was a good job in those days, but it was seasonal, because sugar cane can only be planted and harvested in

the dry season. In those few months, people work long, hard hours and the money they make then runs short before there is work again.

To supplement his income, Melchor Clemente bought an old truck from which he sold groceries and other goods from street to street. He also rented the truck to other people for odd jobs. When things got really tough, Mrs. Clemente worked as a laundress for the family of the sugar company owner, going to work at about midnight, after her family was taken care of and everyone was asleep at home.

Roberto Clemente would later say, "The years of my youth were bad times, but at home we never lacked food and clothing. For my parents, we the children were always first and they came last." He also remembered the warmth of the happy close-knit family being together, talking to one another, telling jokes, laughing. "That was something wonderful," Roberto Clemente said.

As a child, Roberto loved to go to the sugar cane fields with his father, where he could help out and make a few pennies. He had ample opportunity to soak up his father's wisdom during these times together. He told Roberto never to forget where he came from, to be proud of who he was. He'd say Roberto should always help others because "to give is more important than to have."

Certain traits of Roberto Clemente were evident early on. He was considered a serious child with exceptional athletic abilities while in elementary school. He engaged in all sports, baseball being his favorite. Once, his mother said that he was already interested in baseball by age five and that "sometimes he was so much in love with baseball that he did not care for food."

Since he was a well-behaved boy, mindful of his parents, Roberto was never in trouble, except when it came to baseball. He enjoyed telling the following story about himself. At the Clementes, everybody had to be home at a certain time for dinner, but when Roberto was playing baseball time didn't matter to him. When he got home one evening, everybody had eaten, the table had been cleared, and Mrs. Clemente was very unhappy with him.

Roberto said he was sorry, that he had not noticed what time it was because he was playing baseball. Mrs. Clemente, who didn't understand much about sports, said, "Baseball? I'll teach you about baseball." She then grabbed his bat and threw it in the fire of the still-flaming wood-burning stove. Horrified, Roberto retrieved his partly charred bat and promised that he would be more careful from then on — and he was. Years later, when he was already famous, Roberto Clemente would remind his mother about the incident, and she would laugh and say, "But you were never late again, and you did your chores."

Many other stories are told about Clemente's early fascination with baseball. Mr. Clemente would send Roberto to run errands for him in

San Juan, a short bus ride from Carolina. One day he was sent and told to "return quickly." When the bus passed in front of Sixto Escobar Stadium, Roberto got off because a game was on and the San Juan Senators were playing.

In those days, baseball, like much of life, was segregated in the United States. Baseball's excuse was that dark-skinned players were "not good enough." There were separate Negro leagues and leagues where only white men could play. But on the island, even though it had been part of the United States since 1898, no such segregation existed. Black and white players played together in the Puerto Rican Winter Leagues. Monte Irvin, the great slugger of the Negro Leagues (later of the National League's New York Giants), was an outfielder for the San Juan Senators.

The day young Roberto got off that bus, he watched the game from the wire fence. He was spellbound watching real professional baseball, and especially seeing his idol Monte Irvin in action. So much for returning home quickly! Luckily, Mr. Clemente was even-tempered and somewhat understanding of his son's passion, though he didn't know much more than his wife about sports.

After that day, whenever he had a quarter, Roberto spent a dime to go to the stadium and back, and fifteen cents to sit in the bleachers. When the game was over, the youngster would wait for Irvin to leave the stadium. "I never had enough nerve to look at him straight in the face," Clemente recalled. "I would wait for him to pass and then look at him. I idolized him." For Roberto, there was no one like this man who had "arms as big as my legs." Friends in San Antón called Roberto "Monte Irvin" for a while.

In high school, Roberto Clemente was "Most Valuable Player" in track and field, and also excelled in running and javelin throwing, winning medals for both. The all-around athlete was so good with the javelin that he once made a 195-foot throw, an extraordinary feat for a high school student. People hoped he'd represent Puerto Rico in javelin throwing at the Summer Olympics at Helsinki in 1952. But baseball was Clemente's favorite — he was shortstop on the school's all-star team three years in a row — and soon that sport would triumph over all others.

His tenth-grade history teacher, María Isabel Cáceres, said once, "Roberto was a shy boy who always sat in the back of the room. He seldom raised his hand to answer a question. Furthermore, he hardly ever talked, but I was aware that he was smart and had a lot of creative ideas." She also remarked about Roberto, "He had such beautiful hands, huge but gentle. I always looked at them."

Roberto Clemente and his one-time teacher remained lifelong friends. "I will always remember him because once I was sick and he was home from playing baseball and he carried me to the doctor's office in his arms," Mrs. Cáceres said. "When I wanted to pay him, he got mad and said I was insulting him."

The teacher was right about Roberto Clemente being smart. He did well in math and loved working with his hands, building and fixing things. His mother hoped he would be an architect or engineer and help build roads and bridges in Puerto Rico. But whenever she mentioned this, Roberto would say that he thought he "was born to play baseball." Baseball's pull was greater than anything, and his father, knowing how much his son loved the game, suggested that he "play ball and study later."

Those hands his teacher noticed were very consciously exercised. From an early age, Roberto got in the habit of carrying a rubber ball with him a good many hours of the day. Clemente later said, "I would walk to and from school throwing the rubber ball back and forth. Many times at night, I lay in bed and threw the ball against the ceiling and caught it." And when a game was on the radio, he listened to it while throwing the rubber ball at the same time.

María Cáceres was married to Roberto Marín, a rice salesman for Arroz Sello Rojo, or Red Seal. Being a sportsman at heart, he was in charge of the company-sponsored softball team, also called Red Seal. One day, Marín came upon a bunch of boys playing baseball in a sandlot in San Antón. The boys were using sticks for bats and empty cans for balls. He watched them for a while and noticed one who stood out. It was Roberto Clemente.

Red Seal became Roberto Clemente's very first team, and its red-and-white T-shirt his first uniform. At first he played shortstop, but then he played outfield because Marín thought he'd be better there. His powerful arm and brilliant catches began to receive notice. And people laughed when his cap frequently fell off during the game.

"I never saw a boy who liked baseball as he did," Marín said later. "His name became known for his long hits to right field and for his sensational catches." Two other things were noticed about Roberto at the time: He would drink milk and go home immediately when other players hung around drinking beer after the games, and he began developing his own opposite-field batting style.

Two years later, Roberto Clemente played in a tournament and was sensational. This helped confirm his image as an unpolished gem with a strong arm and great speed. Many amateur baseball scouts saw the young player from San Antón and wanted him. Clemente went to play hardball with the amateur Club de Juncos, while still playing softball for Red Seal and baseball for his high school. The quality of the Juncos' players was comparable to Class-A in the professional minor leagues of the mainland.

The moment came when his mentor, Marín, thought that Clemente "looked better than the

professional outfielders" that came to Puerto
Rico for the winter league. Marín took Clemente
to an open tryout for the Brooklyn Dodgers at
Sixto Escobar Stadium. A man who would be
there had a reputation for recognizing raw talent
— he was the one who had found Sandy Koufax.

That man was Al Campanis, the chief talent
scout for the Brooklyn Dodgers in Latin America.
He held open tryouts mainly for their public relations value, and claimed, he'd instead found
most of the talent he'd signed through a sort of
informal network. So, Campanis was bored
watching hopeful after hopeful.

There were seventy-one young men lined up to
make a long throw to home plate from center field
and run the sixty-yard dash. Campanis wasn't
even looking when he heard the loud *pop* the ball
made on contact with the catcher's mitt. Roberto
Clemente had fired the ball on a straight line into
the catcher. "I couldn't believe my eyes," Campanis commented later. "This one kid throws a
bullet, on the fly." Now he was interested. "*¡Uno
más!*" he shouted in Spanish, and Clemente gave
Campanis one more perfect throw.

When Clemente ran the sixty-yard dash, Campanis timed it at 6.4 seconds. The Dodgers' man
yelled again "*¡Uno más!*" and it was 6.4 seconds
again. The scout later said, "The world's record
then was only 6.1. I couldn't believe it!" Campanis was very interested, but suspicious. The kid
could run and throw, but could he hit? The other

hopefuls were sent home and Clemente was given a one-person tryout.

Clemente got into the batting cage and stood far from the plate. The minor-league pitcher working with Campanis that day was told to keep the ball outside. Campanis recalled it well: "He hit line drives all over the place while I'm behind the cage telling myself we got to sign him if he can just hold the bat in his hands. How could I miss him? He was the greatest natural talent I ever saw as a free agent."

Campanis did all he could not to show his excitement about this newfound major-league talent. He would have liked to sign Clemente on the spot, but seventeen-year-old Clemente was legally underage to play professional baseball in the mainland United States. So he told Marín, "He has great tools, but he needs polish."

The coach of the Juncos club was Monchile Concepción, who was also the coach of the professional team the Santurce Crabbers. Marín told Pedrín Zorrilla, the team's owner, about this terrific kid named Clemente.

A week after the conversation Marín had with Zorrilla, the Juncos team went to Manatí, Zorrilla's home town, for an exhibition game. Zorrilla was impressed by a certain player, and asked Concepción who that kid was. Concepción answered, "That boy is from Carolina. They call him 'Momen' and his name is Roberto Clemente." When Zorrilla heard the name, it rang a bell. He took a piece of paper from his pocket, and on reading it, exclaimed, "That's the same boy Roberto Marín recommended to me!"

Marín was pushing for his young protégé, but Zorrilla thought that he shouldn't show too much enthusiasm. If he was to hire Clemente for the Crabbers, he didn't want him to think too much of himself and demand a lot of money. But Zorrilla finally did come around to hiring Clemente.

On October 9, 1952, Roberto Clemente became a professional baseball player for the Santurce Crabbers. He got a $400 bonus and a $40-a-week salary. Zorrilla said he hired Clemente so he could learn "how to put his uniform on right" — no cap falling off while playing. Roberto Clemente was able to continue his studies and received his high school diploma while playing professional baseball.

Zorrilla did not want Clemente to play much right away but to learn by watching the veteran players. He explained later by saying, "I never let the young ones play much. We had great pitchers here. Satchel Paige (future Hall of Famer), pitchers like that . . . A young boy like Clemente strikes out three or four times in a row, he starts asking questions of himself, 'Can I hit? Can I really play?' It's important he does not give himself the wrong answers."

Zorrilla's reasoning was sound, but for Clemente, playing was the one thing that mattered. He only came to bat 77 times, batting .234 that first season, and soon got tired of sitting on the bench. More than once he threatened to quit. Marín told Clemente, "Take it easy, your day will come."

Buster Clarkson, the Crabbers' manager, was the one who saved Clemente's career: "The main thing I had to do was keep his spirits up. He didn't realize how good he was, but I could see his potential. I had three good outfielders, but I had to give him a chance, and he broke into the regular lineup [later] during the first season I managed in Santurce."

Clarkson became "Papa" for Clemente. "I told him he'd be as good as Willie Mays some day. And he was," said the manager who helped polish Clemente. "He had a few rough spots, but he never made the same mistake twice. He had baseball savvy and he listened. He listened to what he was told and he did it."

"Papa" Clarkson helped Clemente correct one of his problems, one that makes a so-called bail-out hitter. That's when a player drags his front foot too much towards the third base line as the pitch comes towards the plate. A little bailing out is considered part of a hitter's style, but a lot is not acceptable. Clemente remembered those days: "Clarkson put a bat behind my left foot to make sure I didn't drag it. He helped me as much as anyone. I was just a kid, but he insisted the older players let me take batting practice."

By the end of the 1952–53 season, Clemente was in the regular lineup of the Crabbers, and at the beginning of the 1953–54 season, he was their regular right fielder. That year, his team won the Puerto Rican championship. They then played against the winner of the Cuban league for the Caribbean title, a title the Crabbers won.

When time came to go to Havana, though, Zorrilla took the veteran players from the Crabbers and a few other veterans from other teams, as he was permitted to do. He left all his younger players at home. Clemente never told Zorrilla how hurt he was, but he told some of his friends. Zorrilla said he knew Clemente never forgave him for not letting him play that game.

At the end of his second season with the Crabbers, Clemente batted .288, with 17 extra-base hits, and 27 RBIs in 219 at-bats. The "gem" was nearly "polished." Major-league teams from the mainland were eyeing him and hoping to sign him up. The Yankees, the Giants, and the Cardinals expressed their interest in him.

Pedrín Zorrilla had started the Crabbers in 1939, when sports were segregated in the U.S. He knew that even outstanding players in the Negro Leagues — U.S.-born and Latin-born blacks — were paid very low salaries. He figured he could hire them cheaply to play in Puerto Rico in the winter along with the best Puerto Rican players. All of this changed after the Brooklyn Dodgers hired Jackie Robinson in 1947 and baseball's color line was no more.

When the winter season ended, Zorrilla called Horace Stoneham, the Giants' owner, to see if he was interested in Clemente. Stoneham was not

— "The kid strikes out too much," he said. Then Zorrilla called the Dodgers.

The Dodgers offered Clemente a $10,000 bonus, and a $5,000 salary for the 1954 season, a fortune for most young people in those days. Other teams were talking to him, too, but there was no argument at the Clementes' about the Dodgers' offer and it was accepted on February 19, 1954.

Almost immediately, the Milwaukee Braves offered Clemente a $28,000 bonus. What should a nineteen-year-old do? He asked his mother, who answered the question plainly and simply, "If you gave your word to one team, you must keep your word." Roberto Clemente consoled himself with the thought that he would be playing for Jackie Robinson's team.

A short time before leaving Puerto Rico, Clemente was involved in a car accident. He had just left the hospital where he was visiting his terminally ill brother when a drunk driver hit Clemente's car and hurt the player's back. The injury would plague him throughout his life.

Roberto Clemente's first stop in the mainland was the Dodgers' spring training camp in Vero Beach, Florida. "He was a free swinger," said Campanis, "and the only thing that concerned us in camp was him standing so far from the plate." Clemente did not go to Brooklyn at the end of spring training. He was sent to the Triple-A Montreal Royals instead, a minor-league team owned by the Dodgers.

The Dodgers were taking a risk and they knew

it. A rule in effect at the time indicated that any player paid a bonus of $4,000 or more could be subjected to a draft by other baseball teams unless he was on the roster of the major-league team for the whole season. The idea behind the draft was to even the quality of all the teams.

The fact that he was sent to Canada did not make Clemente happy. If his English was shaky at best, in Montreal he had to contend with French, a language he understood even less. Also, Canada was so far from home, and not as warm as Puerto Rico, even in the summer.

The actual playing was quite confusing as well. No one knew why certain things were done. "We were playing the first inning," Clemente said, "and I was on my way to the plate with the bases loaded, when suddenly the game was stopped and they sent a pinch hitter up instead of me. Another day I connected for three triples and the next day after that they left me on the bench." Clemente and others thought the behavior of the Royals' manager was crazy at best. Max Macon of the Royals treated him no better than Pedrín Zorrilla had.

Joe Black, who knew Spanish, became Clemente's friend. Black was a powerful Dodger pitcher who was having problems with his arm and was sent to Montreal to get it back into shape. Clemente confided in him that he was so frustrated he was thinking of quitting and going back home.

Black told Clemente that they were hiding him

because of the $4,000 rule. This was even more baffling for Clemente. Either they wanted him or they didn't. His friend told him. "They want you alright, just not yet." Campanis's comment confirms what Black said: "Clemente had superior tools; you didn't have to have a scout to see that."

Clemente threatened to quit and his old mentor, Marín, advised him against it. But Clemente was right — something dirty was going on. When Clemente was no longer in Montreal, a vice president of the Dodgers admitted, "We didn't want the Giants to have Clemente and Willie Mays in the same outfield. It was a cheap deal for us."

In Montreal, Clemente roomed with Chico Fernández in a nice residential neighborhood with a white family that treated them "like human beings." But on the road, in the United States, Clemente felt for the first time the sting of segregation his dark skin brought him. In his homeland in Latin America he had never had to deal with this. In Richmond, Virginia, and other places in the South, the black players had to room in a different hotel from the white players. And they weren't served in the same restaurants, either.

With the Royals, things were also going from bad to worse and Clemente complained constantly. "Some guys thought he was cocky, but he wasn't," Black later said. "He was just having to overcome obstacles, and he would hear things that were said, and they hurt him."

Black said also, "We had a lot of nuts on that

team. They didn't appreciate a black guy who was
a star. They only wanted you to go so far. But the
guys on the team wondered why he wasn't playing. We had to scuffle, and when he played the
second games of doubleheaders, he seemed to
make the difference. But we'd lose and they still
wouldn't play him."

"They tried to make me look bad," Clemente
said of the Royals — but they were not successful.
People from other teams had managed to catch
a glimpse of the man from San Antón. One of
them was Clyde Sukeforth, normally a coach for
the Pittsburgh Pirates, now acting as a scout.

Sukeforth had been sent to Richmond to see
whether Black's arm was better. But he had seen
number 21, an outfielder with a tremendous arm,
during the pregame warmup. Clemente was number 21. Sukeforth later saw him pinch-hit and
then he was absolutely sure. Sukeforth forgot all
about Joe Black. Later in the season, he told
Macon, the Royals' manager, "Take care of our
boy, Max. Make sure nothing happens to him."
After this, the Royals played Clemente even less,
trying to hide him more from the eyes of scouts
from other teams.

The Pirates had been in terrible shape for a
while. At the end of the 1954 season, they were
dead last in the National League, for the third
year in a row. Branch Rickey had been hired to
straighten things out for the Pirates. When Sukeforth described Clemente, Rickey told Howie

Haak, a Pirates' scout, to go to Montreal and take another look.

Macon knew Haak well and knew the reason for that trip to Montreal. While Haak was there, the Royals played Clemente only once. In the last game of the regular season, Clemente was to have played, but when he started walking toward the plate, Macon ordered a pinch hitter to take his place.

That was the last straw for Clemente. He walked out and went back to his hotel to get ready to go back to Puerto Rico. He didn't know that, according to professional baseball rules, if he left at that moment, the Dodgers would have the right to keep him. Haak appeared at Clemente's door when he was packing. Neither one spoke each other's language well, but the message was conveyed.

"You'll end up staying with Brooklyn if you go home," Haak told Clemente. "Finish the year, and next season you'll be playing every day for the Pirates." Clemente listened and unpacked his bags.

In the 1954–55 winter season, Clemente played right field with the Crabbers. The Crabbers' lineup that year is considered one of the best ever assembled anywhere outside the major leagues. Other players in that lineup besides Clemente were Willie Mays, Willie Kirkland, Don Zimmer, George Crowe, Bob Thurman, Sam Jones, and Rubén Gómez. The team won in Puerto Rico and, for the third year in a row, brought home the Caribbean Series title after defeating Venezuela.

Branch Rickey went to Puerto Rico that season to watch Clemente play and liked what he saw. On November 22, 1954, the Pittsburgh Pirates' first draft choice was Roberto Clemente. For $4,000 they acquired him from the Brooklyn Dodgers. Later on, the Dodgers admitted that they had made a big, regrettable mistake. The news reached Clemente in Puerto Rico. "I didn't even know where Pittsburgh was," he said. Roberto Clemente was just what the Pirates needed at that particular moment to revitalize the team.

The fourth game of the 1955 season, the Pirates' new coach, Fred Haney, decided he'd start playing the young talent of the team. Clemente did well against the Dodgers, but his team lost the game. By the eighth game of the season, Clemente was batting .360, but his team had not won a game. Frustration got the best of Clemente and he took it out on the plastic batting helmets, which he shattered with his bat.

When he had broken twenty-two helmets, Haney warned Clemente that if he shattered any more, he'd be charged $10 a piece, a warning that made him stop. Clemente finished that year with a .255 batting average, 23 doubles, and 5 home runs in 124 games. Not too impressive, but he had just turned twenty-one and was still learning.

The first few years of Clemente's Pittsburgh career were tough. He was fined and suspended several times for losing his temper with umpires and others. The once-shy teenager had turned into a very outspoken young man. Clemente said what he felt, decried what he thought was unjust, and did not accept any insults about being Latino or black.

Many in the press corps called Clemente a "hot dog," a derogatory term for a player who is a showoff or does things differently. They also called him a hypochondriac because they said he claimed to be sick all the time. Some of his teammates called him "Jake," a name used for a ballplayer who fakes injuries. But with the fans, the picture was much different. After the games, Clemente would stay in the stadium, mingle with the crowd, and sign autographs. Pittsburgh's fans loved him.

Clemente's health gave him a lot of trouble and sidelined him many times. During the off-season 1956–57 he hurt so much that he had serious thoughts of quitting. He gave himself one more year, and in 1958 he rebounded. That year Clemente played 140 games, batted .289, collected 40 extra-base hits, and recorded 22 assists. That was the first of five times he'd lead the National League in assists. He scored 69 runs and drove in 50 that year. Pittsburgh had 84 wins and placed second, the highest it had been since the early 1940s.

The next year was not as good for Clemente or for the Pirates. He only played 105 games because he had surgery to remove bone chips from his elbow, a remnant of his javelin-throwing days in

high school. The Pirates finished in fourth place
that year.

Off the field, Clemente found life unpleasant in
Pittsburgh. In the North, he encountered prejudice as in the South, although in different guises.
Once, in New York City, he wanted to see a certain set of luggage but the shopkeeper did not
show it to him because "it was too expensive"
and proceeded to show him a less expensive
version.

By 1960, Clemente was playing extremely well
and the Pirates were moving up in the standings.
The Pirates eventually won 95 games and the pennant. That year the Pittsburgh team played the
New York Yankees in the World Series. They were
tied three games apiece when in the seventh game
the Pirates hit a late-inning home run to beat the
"unbeatable" Yankees and win the Series.

Clemente batted .314, with 16 home runs, 89
runs scored, and 94 runs batted in, the most on
the team that year. It was a good year for Clemente, even though he spent five days in the hospital after suffering an accident on the field. He
smashed his face into a concrete wall after making a game-saving catch off Willie Mays. Clemente did not give himself all the credit. "To win,
you must play as a family," he said. "We played
as a family."

Clemente hoped to get the Most Valuable
Player (MVP) award, though. But the sportswriters who voted were against Clemente. A number
of sportswriters were not happy with so many

Hispanic and black players in the major leagues. They refused to call Clemente by his actual first name, Roberto. Instead, they called him Bob or Bobby, which infuriated him. One Pittsburgh writer sent a letter to his colleagues urging them not to vote for Clemente.

The MVP award went to the Pirates' shortstop Dick Groat, who had missed a month of the pennant race due to an injury. Clemente came in eighth place in the voting; he considered this grossly unfair and said so. The sportswriters continued to ignore almost completely what he did in the ballpark through the early 1960s, or gave just a passing mention to it. Clemente was so hurt that he never wore the rings that players on the winning team receive.

In 1961, Clemente was voted to play in the All-Star Game. This meant a lot to him because these voters were the players, coaches, and managers. He felt great in the company of Willie Mays, Frank Robinson, Eddie Mathews, Hank Aaron, and Ernie Banks, and he said so: "The players knew I was most valuable player last year. Then this year they voted me on the All-Star team. I am feeling very good and I will not let them down."

Clemente delivered the winning single as the National League beat the American League, 5 to 4, at Candlestick Park in San Francisco on July 7, 1961.

The year 1961 was a good year for Clemente. That year he recorded his 1,000th career base hit and won his first batting title with a .351 batting average. He also won the first of his twelve Gold Glove awards. He seemed to try harder when he played the Dodgers. Dodger Sandy Koufax wrote about Clemente, *Roberto can hit any pitch, at any time. He will hit pitchouts; he will hit brushback pitches. He will hit high, inside pitches deep to the opposite field, which would be ridiculous even if he didn't do it with both feet off the ground.*

In Puerto Rico, a big party was thrown to celebrate Clemente's 1961 batting championship and for Orlando Cepeda, who was leading in home runs for the New York Giants. This was the first time two Hispanics were leading in two important categories at the same time. The two players traveled together and were received at the airport by a cheering crowd of 18,000 people. At Sixto Escobar Stadium, 5,000 more were there for the official ceremonies. That winter, Clemente had another operation on his elbow.

Early in 1964, Roberto Clemente, self-confident on and off the field, was driving a white Cadillac in San Juan when he saw a lovely young woman. She was going on an errand to a pharmacy. She says, "I noticed that he watched me intently, but I paid no attention and kept walking. When I got to the pharmacy, there he was, reading a newspaper. How he got there before I did, I don't know. Nor do I know why he was there, I only know he was there."

The young woman was Vera Cristina Zabala who was then working as a secretary in a government bank. Roberto Clemente went home and told his mother, "I just met the young woman I am going to marry."

Eight or nine months later, on November 14, 1964, Roberto Clemente and Vera Cristina Zabala were married in the church of San Fernando in Carolina. "Ever since I met him," said his wife, "I knew he was genuine and that he greatly loved all human beings."

Roberto Clemente built a big beautiful house for his bride in the fancy section of Río Piedras in San Juan. The house offered glorious views of the Atlantic Ocean, San Juan Bay, and the mountains. He was a model husband who soon became the father of three boys: Roberto, Jr., Luis, and Enrique. Though Vera Clemente lived with her husband in Pittsburgh when he was there playing, the three children were born in Puerto Rico, as her husband wished.

Between baseball seasons, when Clemente was not playing, the family was in Puerto Rico. Vera Clemente says her husband used to spend hour upon hour playing with the boys, but was not able to discipline them. He also enjoyed playing the organ, fashioning ceramic pieces, and sculpting beautiful things out of driftwood.

One high point followed another in Clemente's career. In 1964, he won a second batting title and in 1965, a third. It was remarkable that the latter happened on a year he suffered a leg injury while mowing the lawn at home, an accident that put him in the hospital for a while. It happened in a year he was also stricken with malaria before spring training, during a trip to the Dominican Republic.

Many people think that 1966 was Roberto Clemente's best year. Even though Clemente did everything humanly possible for his team to win the pennant, the Pirates fell three games short. Although he tried with his usual competitive spirit for the batting championship, the title was won by Dominican-born Matty Alou. But in 1966, Clemente recorded his 2,000th base hit.

It was also in 1966 that Clemente drove in 119 runs and his old enemies, the Baseball Writers of America, voted him the Most Valuable Player. It was a close vote — 218 to 208 — but Clemente won over Sandy Koufax, and that year Koufax had pitched the Dodgers to the pennant.

Roberto Clemente was in Puerto Rico when he heard he'd been voted MVP. His comments were as candid as ever: "When I was a kid, I felt baseball was great to America. They always said Babe Ruth was the best there was, that you would really have to be something to be Babe Ruth, but Babe Ruth was an American player. What we needed was a Puerto Rican player they could say that about, someone to look up to and try to equal."

Roberto Clemente was the first Puerto Rican to be voted MVP. The same day he said, "This makes me happy because now the [Puerto Rican] people feel that if I could do it, then maybe they could do it. The kids have someone to look to and to follow. That's why I like to work with kids so much."

Roberto Clemente had been working with children for many years, setting up several baseball clinics in Puerto Rico to help fight juvenile delinquency.

Like many other ballplayers, Clemente also used to visit sick children in hospitals. But unlike other players, who many times made those visits with photographers sent by their teams, Clemente always went alone. "I do not go because the club wants me to go. I go because I want to go," he'd say. He was also seen giving half-dollar coins to children when walking in poor neighborhoods in Puerto Rico.

Pirates' manager Harry Walker said he thought Clemente was chosen MVP because he did so many little things, "things that some stars don't do: hustling on routine ground balls, breaking up double plays, and hustling to take an extra base." In other words, he set a fine example for other players to follow. The effect Clemente had on the other Pirates players was expressed by catcher Jim Pagliaroni: "When he speaks in the clubhouse and on the field, everyone respects his word."

By 1966, Clemente was truly the model many younger players tried to follow. The younger players idolized him for the rest of his career. For many, he would become a father figure, most notably for Panamanian-born Manny Sanguillén. People started mentioning the Hall of Fame and

Roberto Clemente in the same sentence.

Clemente's relationship with the press corps remained puzzling, though. There was no way the press could continue to ignore him. Even though they voted him MVP in 1966, they frequently made fun of the way he spoke English. Clemente suggested the reporters interview him in Spanish, to see how "intelligent" they sounded.

In 1967, Roberto Clemente won his fourth batting title with a .357 average. That year, the baseball writers said that Roberto Clemente was more valuable to his team than any other player in the league. That year, he signed a contract for $100,000 annually.

Compared with the salaries ballplayers make in the 1990s, $100,000 may not seem a large sum, but it was the first time the Pirates had issued such a contract, and that was the range of salaries made by Willie Mays, Mickey Mantle, Frank Robinson, and Hank Aaron.

In September 1968, Clemente suffered a severe arm injury as he fell backward and rolled downhill, almost 100 feet, at his home in Puerto Rico. It was not a good year for Clemente, nor for the Pirates. Things improved some in 1969, but he reinjured his arm in May while making a diving catch. After that, he tore a thigh muscle slamming into a wall to catch a fly ball.

Clemente heard "boos" from the fans in Pittsburgh in 1969 after grounding into two double plays in two games and making a costly error in right field. "It took me two minutes to realize they

werc booing Clemente," a reporter said. But the
player took it graciously. Clemente tipped his hat
to the fans, and the fans laughed and applauded.

When asked about the incident, Clemente said,
"I wasn't trying to be smart. The fans have always
been kind to me. When I had trouble with my
back in 1956, they were the ones who gave me
the lift I needed. And if they figure I have it coming to me now, then they have the right to boo.
I was just trying to show them that it was all
right with me." Things began to look up later that
year, for Clemente and for the Pirates.

Clemente wore the Pirates' uniform for eighteen years and in that time the team had seven
managers. His relationship with most of them
was often rocky. The managers said Clemente
was hard to get along with. It is more likely that
the managers did not understand him, or his
background, or his culture, nor did they try to.
That has happened a lot with Latin American
players in the major leagues.

But Clemente finally made peace, and even became good friends with manager Danny Murtaugh. Murtaugh came out of retirement to
manage the Pirates a second time in 1970. By
then, Clemente was at his peak. The manager told
Clemente, "When you've got a .340 hitter, you
learn to get along with him." In Clemente's version, what made the change was that Murtaugh
was having back trouble and now understood
what Clemente went through.

Murtaugh said some time later, "There was a

language barrier at the start. Ignorance on both sides. But time took care of that. He was such a truthful man, it backfired on him sometimes. If you asked him if his shoulder hurt, he'd say, 'Yes, it does.' Then he'd go out and throw a guy out at the plate. That's how he got the hypochondriac label." Clemente believed in giving everything he had once he was in uniform, even if he hurt.

Clemente was 441 hits short of 3,000 at the beginning of the 1970 season. "If nothing happens to me, I can do it," Clemente said. "In fact, I could play four more years if I feel like I do right now."

In July 1970, the Pittsburgh Pirates inaugurated their beautiful Three Rivers Stadium in their hometown, two and a half weeks after their last game at their old home, Forbes Field. On July 24, they celebrated "Roberto Clemente Night" at the new stadium before a crowd of 48,846 cheering fans. No other Puerto Rican baseball player had ever received such an honor in the mainland. The event was broadcast by satellite to TV stations outside the United States, another first.

Luisa and Melchor Clemente were on the field with him that night. So were Vera Clemente and their three little boys. The mayor of Carolina and thousands of Puerto Rican fans flew to Pittsburgh just for that night. All the Latin players on the Pirates' roster walked up to Roberto Clemente in single file to embrace him. At the honoree's request, the Pirates donated thousands of dollars to help the crippled children of Pittsburgh's Children's Hospital.

When Roberto Clemente got to the microphone, he was crying. In Spanish, he said, "I want to dedicate this triumph to all the mothers in Puerto Rico. I haven't the words to express my gratitude. I only ask that those who are watching this program be close to their parents, ask for their blessing and embrace."

During the game, in which the Pirates beat the Houston Astros, the fans who came from his homeland sang a song especially written for the occasion, "Roberto Clemente, the pride of Puerto Rico."

That night, Roberto Clemente made a diving catch of a foul ball when the game was easily theirs (11–0) and he injured his knee. He was asked why he risked hurting himself unnecessarily, and he said, "It's the only way I know how to play baseball." Murtaugh took him out of the game, and as Clemente trotted from right field, everyone, including the team's manager, gave him a standing ovation.

In August 1970, Clemente collected ten hits in two days against the Los Angeles Dodgers. In September, he strained his back severely. Clemente wanted to play; Murtaugh wanted him to rest. Times had really changed.

Then came 1971. In January, he was asked to run for mayor of his hometown of Carolina. He listened carefully and finally said, "There's no use in my saying yes. Say I was elected and a situation came up where I have to compromise. I cannot compromise."

The Baseball Writers of Houston, Texas, gave an award to Clemente just before the 1971 season. He delivered "the most inspirational speech we've ever had," said a participant. In that speech, Clemente said, "Accomplishment is something you can't buy. Any time you have the opportunity to accomplish something for somebody who comes behind you and you don't do it, you are wasting your time on this earth."

In 1971, the Pittsburgh Pirates won the National League pennant and went on to defeat the heavily favored Baltimore Orioles in the World Series in seven thrilling games. Clemente's batting average was .414. He was voted MVP again.

After the game, Roberto Clemente began a TV interview with these words: "Before I say anything, I want to say something in Spanish to my mother and father." The elder Clementes were in Puerto Rico watching their son on TV in the comfortable house he had bought for them years before. "On this, the proudest day of my life, I ask for your blessing," he told them.

That winter, Roberto Clemente received many awards in various parts of the country. And through it all, he paid homage to his fellow Latin and black baseball players: "My greatest satisfaction comes from helping to erase the old opinion about Latin Americans and blacks. People never questioned our ability, but they considered us inferior to their station in life. Simply because many of us were poor, we were thought to be low class."

By 1972, Roberto Clemente's dream of building a "sports city" in his homeland had already taken shape in his mind. "It's the biggest ambition in my life," he said. He envisioned baseball fields, swimming pools, basketball and tennis courts as well as other recreational activities. He wanted a place open to everybody, rich or poor, where families could play together.

The quest for the 3,000 hits was still going on at the beginning of September 1972. Clemente needed only 25 more to achieve that goal.

On September 30, at 3:07 in the afternoon, Roberto Clemente became the eleventh player in the history of baseball to get 3,000 hits. The umpire handed the historic ball to the star and the crowd cheered wildly for a full minute. Clemente said simply, "I dedicate this hit to the fans of Pittsburgh and to the people of Puerto Rico and to the person I owe the most in professional baseball, Roberto Marín."

On December 23, 1972, an earthquake of enormous proportions destroyed much of the city of Managua, Nicaragua, and killed and injured thousands of people. In Puerto Rico, Roberto Clemente and two friends, TV producer Luis Vigoreaux, and singer Ruth Fernández, started a committee to send relief to the victims.

The committee sent money and two planeloads of medicine, clothing, and food, but reports came back that the victims were not getting everything that was meant for them because some of the supplies were being stolen. "If I go to Nicaragua, the stealing will stop. They would not dare to steal from Roberto Clemente," he said.

Roberto Clemente decided to go to Nicaragua on New Year's Eve. Vera Clemente wanted him to wait until after New Year's but he said, "It's the least I can do. Babies are dying over there. They need the supplies." He assured his wife it would be a short trip and asked her to have his favorite festive dishes ready for his return.

Vera Clemente drove her husband to the airport. A chartered plane, an old DC-7, was supposed to take off at four P.M. but due to mechanical problems it did not leave as scheduled. Vera Clemente kissed her husband good-bye at five and went to meet some friends who were coming from Pittsburgh.

The plane finally took off at 9:22 P.M. with five people on board. A loud explosion occurred minutes after takeoff, and one of the four engines caught fire. The pilot could not return to the airport because two more explosions sent the plane into the Atlantic Ocean.

The search for the men began immediately but only the body of the pilot was recovered. Professional divers, relatives, and friends searched for the others. Teammate Manny Sanguillén searched in the water after the others had given up. Of Roberto Clemente, only his briefcase was found.

The entire island of Puerto Rico went into shock. Church bells tolled and the governor declared three days of official mourning. The entire

Pirates team flew to the island to pay their respects.

In January 1973, just days after his death, the president of the Baseball Writers of America called for a special meeting to discuss Roberto Clemente's induction into the Hall of Fame. According to the rules, a player has to be retired from the game for five years to be eligible for the Hall of Fame. But the rule was waived in Clemente's case.

On March 20, it was announced that Clemente had received 393 votes, 75 more than needed, to become a member of the Hall of Fame. The 29 people who voted against said they wanted Clemente in, but five years later, because they were afraid a precedent might be set.

On opening day, April 6, 1973, the Pirates retired Clemente's number 21 before a crowd of 51,095 fans. No other Hispanic baseball player had been given that honor before. The scoreboard at Three Rivers Stadium read *Thank you, Roberto. We will never forget the Great One.* The Pirates have kept their word. Every year they dedicate one night to him. And at least three awards in the world of baseball carry his name.

On August 6, 1973, Vera and other members of the Clemente family were in Cooperstown, New York. Roberto Clemente was inducted into the Baseball Hall of Fame, the first Hispanic so immortalized, on the same day Monte Irvin, the idol of his youth, was inducted. This was Roberto Clemente's final and most lasting achievement.

Only Baby Ruth had been inducted into the Hall of Fame in less than the required five years.

There are many biographies of Roberto Clemente published to date. The first was published when he was still alive. Some are in English, some are in Spanish, and one of the most recent ones is in Japanese. Countless other books about baseball have chapters on Roberto Clemente.

The U.S. Postal Service issued a Roberto Clemente stamp in 1984, the first Hispanic player to appear on such a stamp, the fourth sports personality to receive the honor. No one seems to know the exact number of schools, playgrounds, and other institutions named after him.

Vera Clemente is the undisputed chief keeper of her husband's memory and dream. After a period of deep mourning, she vowed to continue Clemente's work for his sports complex. She mobilized the authorities, private businesses, and the general public.

Roberto Clemente Sports City sits today on land the star baseball player had bought, on the outskirts of Carolina, a few miles from San Juan's airport. *The Sports City's main purpose*, reads one of its brochures, *is to create better citizens through sport, recreation and cultural activities*.

The complex has facilities for jogging, riding, volleyball, soccer, gymnastics, judo, golf, baseball, basketball, boxing, swimming, tennis, archery, camping, and cycling. There are parks, dormitories, and cafeterias, as well as a museum, a chapel, an auditorium, and several statues and monuments. What has been built so far has cost $13 million, and there are plans to add more facilities. Classes of various kinds are held throughout the day Monday to Saturday, for children from three to eighteen years of age. There are special classes for children with disabilities.

Today, the director of Sports City bears a familiar name, Roberto Clemente, Jr.

5
Vilma S. Martínez

Many years ago in the southwestern United States there were signs in barbershops reading NO MEXICANS OR DOGS ALLOWED. Similar signs were common in all sorts of establishments including public swimming pools and certain parks. The term "Mexican" was used to refer to people of Mexican descent, even if they were born in the United States, and therefore American citizens.

Scores of Chicanos, persons of Mexican descent or Mexican-Americans, recall with sadness the times they were not invited to a white classmate's birthday party because of prejudice. Many also recall that when they spoke Spanish at school, they were scolded by a teacher, or hit, or both.

If a boy was born in San Antonio, Texas, in 1943 and his parents were poor and had a Spanish surname, he faced enormous problems as he grew up. If a girl was born, she faced the same problems and more. It took a lot of courage, determination, and hard work to overcome those problems. One who beat the odds is a prominent attorney named Vilma Martínez.

Vilma's father, Salvador Martínez, was a good student in high school and wanted to get a football scholarship to go to college, but because he was Mexican he didn't get the scholarship. That meant he didn't have the money to go to college. He married Nena Piña, a young woman who only finished the seventh grade, and together they started a family. The first of their five children, a girl, was born on October 17, 1943, in San Antonio, Texas. She was named Vilma Socorro Martínez.

Good paying jobs were not easy to get for Salvador Martínez, so the family struggled. Vilma was taught at home to read and write in Spanish by her paternal grandmother. In elementary school, Vilma made excellent grades from the start, and by the time she was in sixth grade, she skipped a grade. "We wanted to do it earlier," a friendly teacher told her about the grade-skipping, "but the principal didn't let us." It was allowed only when the school got a new principal.

In junior high school, Vilma Martínez made straight A's and was thinking of college. When she told her counselor to send her papers to Jefferson, the academic high school, the counselor told her, "You'd be more comfortable going to Fox, the vocational high school. That's where all

Mexicans go." Young Vilma answered back
firmly, "I don't want to be comfortable. I want
to go to college. Please send my papers to Jefferson."

A little Chicana was supposed to be meek and
accepting. Martínez says of the incident, "The
counselor was shocked, but did it." Martínez
adds, "In those days, the highest aspiration of
most Mexican-American girls was to be a secretary."

At Jefferson High School, Vilma Martínez made
straight A's and became the treasurer of the
school's honor society. But when she asked the
counselor to help her get the college application
forms, the counselor was always busy. "Every
time I approached the counselor, she would tell
me, 'Later,' " Martínez recalls. "I am very stub-
born and would not be discouraged, so I wrote to
the University of Texas [in Austin] by myself and
got the forms."

Meanwhile, a battle was going on at home, too.
Salvador Martínez did not want his daughter to
go to college. For one thing, girls were supposed
to get married, have children, and stay home.
That was the way many men of his generation
and background thought. Also, the university was
in a different town. In his opinion, a young girl
shouldn't be there alone. "I got my litigation
skills from the arguments I had with my father,"
Martínez says.

Vilma Martínez decided that words alone
would not solve anything and she had to go out

and prove that she could do it. That's why neither
an unhelpful counselor nor a disapproving father
stopped Vilma Martínez from attending college.
She graduated from the University of Texas in
1964, completing a four-year program in just two-
and-a-half years. Being the oldest child, "I was
too scared that something would happen to my
father and I would have to go back home to work
full time to help the family," Martínez says. She
also worried that she might not get enough
money to pay for her studies for a longer period
of time.

At age fifteen, Vilma Martínez had worked as
a general office helper for Alonzo Perales, a San
Antonio lawyer. She knew she had the ability to
be a lawyer, too. Shortly after arriving at the
University of Texas, Martínez told a counselor she
wanted to go to law school. The counselor told
her, "You have to have *very good* grades to go to
law school." The next time they met, Martínez,
showing her outstanding grades, asked the counselor, "Are these grades good enough?" The counselor replied, "Don't get your hopes too high . . .
they are *very* selective."

Martínez was wondering what to do as she
washed dishes at the lab where she was working,
and told the teacher at the lab about the situation.
The teacher said, "You should apply to one of the
big liberal eastern schools." Martínez grabbed a
pencil and paper and said, "Tell me the names
of those schools." The teacher gave Martínez a
few names and she wrote to some of the schools.

When she got her University of Texas diploma, Vilma Martínez went home and told her father, "You see this degree? I can do it." Then she said she was going to law school on the East Coast. Her father offered to pay for her studies if she stayed in a San Antonio law school, but his daughter declined the offer. "You are breaking your mother's heart by going so far away," Mr. Martínez told his daughter. Vilma asked her mother if what her father had said was true, and Mrs. Martínez told her, "If you are happy, I am happy. You are not breaking my heart."

Vilma Martínez went to Columbia University Law School in New York City but she was also accepted at the University of Texas Law School. Being an honor graduate of the University of Texas, admission to their law school was no problem. "But I was fed up," Martínez says, "so I went to New York City."

The personal battle for equality continued in New York, but now it was more for being a woman than for being a Chicana. At the beginning of her first semester at Columbia University Law School, Martínez applied for a prestigious fellowship. The interviewer told her, "Why should we give you the money if you're going to get married and have children and not practice law?" Martínez replied, "If I had wanted to get married and have children, I would have done it already. I haven't worked this hard not to practice law." She got that fellowship, and after that, she got other scholarships and worked at a variety of part-time jobs to pay for her studies.

There were 300 students in Martínez's fresh-
man class at Columbia University Law School,
out of which only 25 were women. Martínez was
the only Mexican-American in the entire group.
Of her law school years, she has said that it was
wonderful to be considered solely for her abilities. She received her law degree in 1967.

Her first job, right after graduation, was as staff
attorney for the National Association for the Ad-
vancement of Colored People [NAACP] Legal Defense Fund in New York City. She did civil rights
litigation and became involved with the Mexican-
American Legal Defense and Educational Fund
[MALDEF] from its beginning. The stories of
MALDEF and Vilma Martínez cannot be told
apart from each other.

Pete Tijerina, a lawyer from Texas, was the
guiding force behind MALDEF. He was a member
of the League of Latin American Citizens Foundation [LULAC] and, by the 1960s, had been ac-
tively fighting discrimination for a long time.

Tijerina talked to Hispanic students to make
them see the need for education and for learning
English. He raised money for scholarships. He
spoke out against local racist policies. He inves-
tigated crimes when racial motivations were suspected. He talked to politicians about correcting
school segregation problems. His work was ex-
emplary, but limited to his own state of Texas.

In April 1966, Tijerina was in Jourdanton,
Texas, representing a Mexican-American woman

who had lost her right leg at the knee in an accident. He thought the woman should receive $50,000 in compensation, but the other party disagreed. Tijerina decided to take the case to trial but changed his mind when he realized there were no Spanish-surnamed people on the jury panel.

Tijerina knew very well that, in those days, it was common for Southwest Anglos to think that "Mexicans don't need much money to live on." Under those circumstances, the case would almost certainly be lost. He talked to a judge and the judge told him to come back in August, that there would be some Hispanic people on the jury panel by then.

In the summer, Tijerina was invited by Jack Greenberg to attend a meeting of the NAACP Legal Defense Fund in Chicago. He couldn't go, but he sent an associate in his place. The associate told Tijerina upon his return that the Legal Defense Fund was doing wonderful things on behalf of African-Americans.

In August, Tijerina returned to Jourdanton to find out there were only two Spanish names to select from the jury panel. One had been dead for ten years; the other was a person who, being an alien and not a U.S. citizen, could not serve on a jury. Tijerina had to settle the case for a much smaller amount than he felt the woman deserved.

This case was much too painful for Tijerina to bear and he talked about it with fellow lawyers and activists in San Antonio. They discussed a

number of possible actions they could take and
finally settled on one.

In the spring of 1967, Tijerina traveled to New
York City with two associates. They had a meeting with Bill Pincus of the Ford Foundation.

After the men made their presentation, Pincus
said the Ford Foundation was willing to consider
a proposal to form a Mexican-American Legal Defense Fund, using the NAACP Legal Defense Fund
as a model. The main office was to be established
in Texas and regional offices would be set up in
New Mexico, Arizona, California, and Colorado.
The NAACP Legal Defense Fund helped them get
a small grant from the Field Foundation to do
the preliminary work of writing the proposal.

Tijerina and his secretary worked long hours
gathering information for the proposal that had
to be written. In the summer, Tijerina and his
family traveled throughout the five southwestern
states to form local committees.

In the fall of 1967, the NAACP Legal Defense
Fund helped by sponsoring a conference in Ban-
dera, Texas, for Chicano lawyers from all over the
country who were interested in civil rights. A
MALDEF publication states, "Among the participants was a young Chicana named Vilma Socorro Martínez, who was working as an attorney
for [NAACP] LDF and who began serving as an
important liaison with the budding civil rights
organization [MALDEF]."

A significant event took place in Vilma Martínez's personal life in 1968 — she married Stuart

Singer, a fellow lawyer she had met at a bar review class. All students who graduate from law schools must pass a difficult examination in order to be admitted to the bar, or the legal profession. Each state has its own bar and a lawyer has to pass a different exam in every state where he or she wants to practice. Vilma Martínez is a member of the New York State Bar and the California Bar, having passed these two states' tests, both considered among the most difficult. She is also qualified to appear before the U.S. Supreme Court, something not all lawyers who pass the bar exam can do.

Early in 1968, Tijerina was able to announce publicly that his group was seeking a $1 million grant to create a civil rights organization. Vilma Martínez had helped write the proposal. On May 1, 1968, representatives from all the committees in the five southwestern states met in San Antonio with Bill Pincus.

Pincus told the participants that the Ford Foundation was giving them $2.2 million — more than double their request — to be spent over the next five years for civil rights legal work for Mexican-Americans. Of that money, $250,000 was to be used for scholarships for Chicano law students because the Ford Foundation realized there were not enough Mexican-American lawyers. In addition, the ones already in practice did not have the income or the experience to work on civil rights. The NAACP Legal Defense Fund offered its continuing support.

MALDEF's first office opened in San Antonio on
August 1, 1968. Tijerina was chosen as the organ-
ization's first executive director. Mario Obledo, a
Texas assistant attorney general and former LU-
LAC state director, was hired as general counsel.

Vilma Martínez worked at the NAACP Legal
Defense Fund and served as its in-house liaison
with MALDEF until 1970. One of her commit-
ments to MALDEF was to find foundations that
might offer financial backing for the struggling
organization. The job was difficult because in the
opinion of many of the foundations, Chicanos had
a problem only in the Southwest.

Martínez would then tell the skeptics that the
problems of African-Americans started in the
South and spread throughout the country. Chicanos and Latinos in general faced a similiar situation, she said. With that type of reasoning she
was able to raise a lot of money for MALDEF.

In 1970, Vilma S. Martínez and another Chicana attorney, Grace Olivarez, became the first
female members of the Board of Directors of
MALDEF. That year, Martínez went to work for
the New York State Division of Human Rights as
equal opportunity counsel. For the state of New
York, she helped draft and implement new regulations and administrative procedures on employment rights.

Meanwhile, MALDEF's offices became "the law
firm of the poor." Small cases flooded the organization, cases that were "routine" and could be
handled by any lawyer. MALDEF's original in-

tention was to deal with big important cases that would make it possible for existing laws to be changed or new laws to be passed. The way things stood, this was not happening. There were also differences of opinion among the people who worked for the organization. Something had to be done if MALDEF was to survive.

In May 1970, Obledo became MALDEF's new executive director, while retaining his duties as general counsel. The main office was moved from San Antonio, Texas, to San Francisco, California. Under Obledo's leadership, MALDEF began to work more at a national than local level.

In 1971, Vilma Martínez applied for a job at Cahill, Gordon & Reindel, a Wall Street law firm in New York City. During the interview, she was asked, "What makes you think that you can do this job, with your NAACP experience?" Never at a loss for words, Martínez responded, "Rules are rules." She got the job and became a litigation associate, arguing cases in court.

At Cahill, Gordon & Reindel, Martínez did federal and state court civil litigation. By now she didn't have to hear stupid remarks like "You're awfully bright — for a Mexican," and she was happy about that. But even here she felt the sting of discrimination, as a woman. Whenever Vilma Martínez went to court with a male colleague, he was always treated as a lawyer, while she was likely to be treated as his secretary. And when her law firm gave a party at an exclusive men's club, Martínez refused to attend. The club would not allow a woman to enter through the main entrance but only through a side door.

In 1973, MALDEF's director resigned from his job to go into private practice. Vilma Martínez had been grumbling about the way business was being conducted at MALDEF. When the vacancy occurred, Martínez's husband asked her, "Why don't you apply?" She applied and lobbied, and with her reputation as a top-notch litigation attorney already established, she got the job.

Vilma S. Martínez became MALDEF's president and general counsel in September 1973. She immediately set out to make big changes. A MALDEF office was opened in Washington, D.C., to improve the organization's government relations, funding sources, and national visibility. Next was the creation of specialized litigation and educational projects.

Education has always been important for MALDEF. From the beginning, the organization has been in favor of bilingual education and has been involved in several cases dealing with this controversial issue. Under Martínez, MALDEF sued California's state schools superintendent to ensure that bilingual education laws were obeyed.

One of the new projects was the Chicana Rights Project to fight sex discrimination against Mexican-American women. Another was a program to help train and assist Mexican-American lawyers interested in practicing in certain communities.

Among the most important things MALDEF

has done is to make sure the organization only got involved in the big cases with the greatest impact, as it had been originally intended. For example, MALDEF filed a suit because many school districts in Texas refused to enroll the children of undocumented aliens unless their parents paid tuition. No one else paid tuition in those public schools, the organization argued. Why should only some of the parents pay?

"How can we deny education to any child?" Martínez says. "Maybe one of those children can [grow up and] find a cure for cancer or another disease." The U.S. Supreme Court agreed with MALDEF. Now no one has to pay tuition to attend public schools anywhere.

Legal observers point out that during Martínez's nine years with the organization, the level of expertise in civil rights matters among the staff she hired markedly increased, and most of those employees were Chicanos. Some of the young lawyers were the products of MALDEF programs or had gotten MALDEF scholarships.

Because of MALDEF's work, certain important reforms were made by the Census Bureau in its census-taking procedures. Martínez played a key role by advising the Census Bureau prior to the 1980 census. During the Carter administration, she also served on a committee to choose ambassadors to represent the United States in other countries.

On the personal side of things, Stuart Singer left New York and found a job in California to be

closer to his wife. But his office was in Los Angeles
and hers in San Francisco, so she moved to Los
Angeles, too, and commuted to work in San
Francisco.

Also, during this time of intense professional
activity, Vilma Martínez gave birth to two sons,
four years apart, named Carlos Singer and Ri-
cardo Singer, signifying their dual heritage. Martínez's husband was Jewish, born in the United
States.

Martínez recalls that a Los Angeles neighbor
once saw her pushing a baby stroller. He com-
plimented her on her "good English," thinking
she was the maid. "I told him most graduates of
Columbia Law School have good English."
Surely she said it with a smile because she always
remembers a bit of advice her mother gave her
long ago. Anger and bitterness only make a person unhappy, Mrs. Martínez said to her daughter,
and if you yell, nobody will hear what you have
to say. That's why people often remark that Vilma
Martínez is a tough lady with a sweet smile who
never ever raises her voice.

In 1982, Martínez resigned from MALDEF's top
spot. She said that "personally and professionally
it was time to move on." When she started, MAL-
DEF had a budget of $800,000 a year; when she
left, it was $2.6 million.

The list of MALDEF's accomplishments during
Martínez's tenure is longer, but that's not all she
did. Martínez believes strongly that "you can

only accomplish so much if you join hands with those from your own background." She believes in diversification. That's why she works with Japanese-American groups, the Congressional Black Caucus, organized labor, and others.

In 1982, Vilma Martínez became a litigation partner at the prestigious law firm of Munger, Tolles & Olson in Los Angeles. She does federal and state court civil litigation. She deals with cases of wrongful termination of a job and employment discrimination.

Vilma Martínez remains committed to helping the Hispanic community and other minorities. That's why she is a board member of numerous organizations with that aim and she rejoined MALDEF's board in 1992.

A very important appointment Vilma Martínez had was as a member of the Board of Regents of the University of California, from 1976 to 1990, a group she chaired from 1984 to 1986. To her, being a regent meant a lot. As she has said, "Many people are interested in power and money . . . but what intrigues me most is knowledge."

Vilma Martínez has been invited to speak at dozens of places all over the country and overseas. She has spoken to undergraduate college students and professors, to law school students, to newspaper reporters, to advertising agency personnel, and many others.

To date, Vilma Martínez has received numerous awards, including Honorary Doctor of Laws,

Amherst College; Distinguished Alumnus Award, University of Texas; and Medal for Excellence, Columbia Law School.

When asked what she is most proud of, Vilma Martínez says that she is very proud of having helped MALDEF become an institution, of her work so that the Voting Rights Act includes Mexican-Americans, and of all the work done in Texas.

She is just as proud of her thirteen years as a member of the University of California Board of Regents. And she loves being a practicing attorney, which she is today.

Being the mother of her two sons gives her special pride. In an article about California's "most powerful lawyers," it was noted that Martínez is the only one on that list who is raising a young family while working as a lawyer.

Bridging the two cultures that are part of her life is important to her, too, because "both cultures have enormous strengths." Immigrants, says Martínez, make this country renew and define its culture, and "that's very exciting."

Education gives knowledge and a ticket out of poverty, Martínez says. That's why she likes to tell young people "to follow their dream, be prepared to work hard, and persevere."

It seems certain that Vilma S. Martínez, "the quiet and effective fighter for Mexican-American rights," and for all people's rights, will keep following her dream, working hard, persevering as she always has. No doubt, she will accomplish much more than she has already achieved. And it is quite likely that she will receive more recognition in years to come.

6
Antonia C. Novello

The first woman to become "the nation's doctor," as she likes to say, needed extensive medical care herself for a number of years. A birth defect dogged Toñita Coello up until she was in college, but it did not prevent her from reaching her goals. For one thing, she says, "*Mami* never treated me as a sick child"; for another, she's always thought that "If life gives you a lemon, you make lemonade." That's Dr. Antonia Coello Novello in a nutshell. (Toñita is a nickname for Antonia; Novello is her married name.) She does not allow obstacles and difficulties to overpower her.

Antonia Coello was born in Fajardo, a small coastal town thirty-two miles from San Juan, Puerto Rico, on August 23, 1944. She was the oldest child of Ana Delia and Antonio Coello, who died when Toñita was eight years old. Her mother later married Ramón Flores, "the only father I ever knew, really," Dr. Novello says.

Ana Delia Coello Flores has worked in the schools a lifetime, first as a teacher and then as a principal — fifty years in 1993 and still working. "*Mami* used to take me to school when I was a little girl because there was no baby-sitter," Dr. Novello says. "In those days there was no kindergarten in Fajardo. *Mami* would sit me in the first grade so I could be with other kids. By the time I was five, the teachers told *mami* at the end of the school year, 'Put her in the second grade, she already knows how to read and write.' "

All this happened before Toñita Coello's first operation for an intestinal disease. She had to be seen very frequently by pediatricians (children's specialists) and gastroenterologists (stomach and intestines' specialists). She also had to stay in the hospital at least two weeks every summer. "My doctors became my buddies," Dr. Novello says. "I wanted to be like them, caring and reassuring, but I didn't tell anybody about that."

Quietly, Toñita began thinking of being a pediatrician, to help other children so they wouldn't suffer as much as she did. The nurse who took care of her, an aunt she called *mami Loli*, would say to everyone who'd listen, "This one is going to be a doctor." Her aunt had figured it out.

The only way to cure her particular condition was surgery, and Toñita Coello was to have had the operation at age eight. "But somehow," says Dr. Novello, "somebody forgot. I fell through the cracks," and the operation was not performed. "In those days, people didn't question the doctors; you accepted whatever they said," she adds.

The tough little girl sailed through school — at age ten she was in the seventh grade and made excellent marks with all her teachers, including her mother, who taught her math and science that year. As a high school junior, she took the Advanced Placement trigonometry test to get college credit. "I could take it again the following year if I didn't pass it that time," Dr. Novello says. When the results were known, the teacher called her in and told her, "Toñita, you had the highest grade!"

"Until then, I didn't think I was smart," says Dr. Novello. "Before that I thought I was getting good grades because all the teachers knew my mother." But Antonia Coello earned her good marks on her own merits, and graduated with high honors.

At the University of Puerto Rico in Río Piedras, Antonia Coello received a bachelor of science degree in 1965, even while suffering her share of physical pain. Between her sophomore and junior years in college, when she was eighteen, Antonia Coello had had enough of her chronic illness and insisted on having the operation. But the only doctor in Puerto Rico who was willing to do the procedure was a cardiovascular surgeon, whose speciality was operating on the heart and blood vessels, not the intestines.

After the surgery, complications arose. One

of her professors made arrangements for her to
go to the Mayo Clinic in Minnesota, one of the
most highly regarded medical institutions in the
United States. "I didn't know anything about the
Mayo Clinic then," Dr. Novello says. She spent
two months being treated there and has nothing
but praise for the clinic and the doctors who took
care of her.

Her aunt, the nurse, suffered from kidney ailments. When Antonia Coello was at the Mayo
Clinic, her aunt died of a kidney disease. Dr. Novello says, "Now I knew I should also be a nephrologist" (kidney specialist).

Without telling anyone, Antonia Coello applied
and got accepted to the University of Puerto Rico
Medical School, also in Río Piedras. She was
going to be a medical doctor, and a pediatrician,
to help kids. She was going to be a nephrologist,
too, to help people with kidney disease.

That's what Antonia Coello desired deep down
inside. She tried to reassure herself, but she was
also frightened. Though she had already proven
that she could succeed, she was afraid she might
fail. Also, there was the matter of money — there
wasn't too much of it at home to pay for more
years of schooling. That's why Antonia Coello told
her family about her dreams only after being accepted by the medical school. Mrs. Flores told her
daughter, "If there's a bank where you're going,
you'll be fine. We'll get loans. We'll find the way."

So it was that the young woman from Fajardo
who defeated a serious illness became Dr. An-

tonia Coello in 1970, and in the process was elected to Alpha Omega Alpha, the national honorary medical society. The same year she married Dr. Joseph Novello, a navy flight surgeon who was stationed in Fajardo at the time.

Drs. Antonia and Joseph Novello then traveled to Ann Arbor, Michigan, to continue their medical training at the University of Michigan. He went on to specialize in psychiatry while she went on to specialize in pediatrics, as she always knew she would.

Dr. Antonia C. Novello did her internship and residency in pediatrics at the University of Michigan, from 1970–73, and was selected intern of the year her first year on the job. She then specialized further, in pediatric nephrology, at the University of Michigan, in 1974, and at Georgetown University, in Washington, D.C., in 1975.

In 1976, Dr. Antonia C. Novello started her own private practice as a pediatric nephrologist in Springfield, Virginia, but two years later she closed the office. She has been quoted again and again as saying that "when the pediatrician cries as much as the parents of the patients do, then you know it's time to get out." Dr. Novello thought that she could help kids better somewhere else.

Soon Dr. Novello learned of an opening for a pediatrician in the U.S. Navy. She was familiar with the service because her husband was a navy man. But when she applied, a captain, with his feet on his desk, gave her a rather disrespectful

look and said, "Don't you know we are looking
for a few good *men*?" Dr. Novello left without
saying a word, and in the office across the street,
she found out they were looking for doctors to
work in the United States Public Health Service.
She applied and got a job immediately. "Oh, I
know that when one door closes, another one
opens for you," Dr. Novello says.

In 1978, Dr. Antonia C. Novello went to work
as a project officer in the artificial kidney program
at the National Institutes of Health. Then, quietly, "when nobody was paying any attention to
me," she says, "I went back to school." In 1982
she received a master's degree in public health,
with a special study emphasis in health services
administration, from Johns Hopkins University
in Maryland.

She worked with the Senate Committee on Labor
and Human Resources for eighteen months and
contributed in substantial ways to the drafting and
passing into law of the National Organ Transplant
Act of 1984. This law established a national network
for acquiring human organs for transplantation,
finding the tissue type of the organs, locating where
they are found, and transporting them to the
compatible patients who need them.

While a legislative fellow, Dr. Antonia C. Novello also helped draft labels warning of health
risks associated with smoking. Those labels are
currently used on cigarette packages and in other
advertising materials.

In 1986, Dr. Antonia C. Novello was named deputy director of the National Institute of Child Health and Human Development. One of her numerous responsibilities was coordinating pediatric AIDS research. In addition, Dr. Novello served as co-chair of the Advisory Committee on Women's Health Issues. She was also charged with the responsibility of direction and administration of extramural health programs. These are health-related programs backed by the National Institutes of Health conducted in universities and other institutions.

In 1986, Dr. Antonia C. Novello added another responsibility to her heavy load, that of clinical professor of pediatrics at the Georgetown University School of Medicine. Later she also began teaching pediatrics at the Uniformed Services University of the Health Sciences.

In the summer of 1987, Dr. Novello was selected to attend the Program for Senior Managers in Government at the John F. Kennedy School of Government at Harvard University in Massachusetts.

Then, in 1989 came the event that made Dr. Novello famous. She was chosen to be Surgeon General of the United States.

The Surgeon General advises the public on health matters, such as smoking and health, AIDS, diet and nutrition, environmental hazards, and the importance of immunization and disease prevention. The office also supervises the activities of 6,400 members of the Public Health Service.

"I wasn't involved in politics," Novello says. "I was very surprised when I was first called. In fact, I thought it was a joke. I hung up the phone." But she was called again because the offer was serious.

The selection was made official by President George Bush on October 17, 1989. Before her Senate confirmation hearings, Dr. James A. Sammons, the executive vice president of the American Medical Association, said that Dr. Novello's qualifications for the job of Surgeon General were "outstanding and impeccable." She was superbly qualified not only as a physician but as a health services administrator. After routine background information, the confirmation process went through the Senate smoothly.

Radiant and resplendent, in the uniform of vice admiral of the U.S. Navy (Every U.S. Surgeon General can choose to wear the uniform of any branch of the armed forces.), flanked by her mother and her husband, Dr. Antonia C. Novello took the oath of office at a ceremony in the White House on March 9, 1990. She became the first female, as well as the first Hispanic, ever to serve as Surgeon General of the United States. The oath was administered by another "first," Justice Sandra Day O'Connor, the first female in the U.S. Supreme Court, while President Bush and Dr. Louis Sullivan, Secretary of Health and Human Services, looked on.

Just by being a member of an ethnic minority and a woman, Antonia C. Novello brought a certain understanding to her job that was not always present in that office when it came to problems of minorities and women. "Women learn to be diplomatic and to listen," she says.

From her unique perspective of having suffered a debilitating chronic illness up until her college days, Dr. Antonia C. Novello also brought into sharp focus the problems of children and youth.

One example of her insights can be seen in an article Dr. Novello wrote for *Hispanic* magazine:

Too often, the term "Hispanic" is used simplistically, referring broadly to all populations with ancestral ties to Spain, Latin America, or the Spanish-speaking Caribbean. Such uncritical ethnic labeling can and may obscure the diversity of social histories and cultural identities that characterize these populations and, in turn, can influence health behaviors, the way care is accessed, and ultimately, health outcomes.

Dr. Novello explains further that the health needs of Puerto Rican communities in the United States are different from those of Central and South Americans who may be fleeing a war-torn country. She also believes the needs of fifth-generation Mexican-Americans are entirely different from the needs of recent Mexican immigrants.

Dr. Novello has addressed all aspects of health

in the country. About farm health, she has said, "These [farm] workers and their families experience a disproportionate share of injuries and diseases associated with chemical, biological, and physical hazards." To that effect, she suggested, "Injuries need to be viewed as a public health problem — allowing us to deal with them the same way we approach disease prevention."

The Surgeon General was also involved with a conference called "Healthy Children Ready to Learn" for parents, educators, medical and social service providers, and community leaders and officials from all states and the federal government. The purpose of the gathering was to find ways to work together to solve a long list of problems that prevent children from learning.

Numerous studies about the health of Hispanics — who suffer higher rates of diabetes, high blood pressure, and some types of cancer than other ethnic groups — have been conducted due to Dr. Novello's interest.

Every doctor who becomes Surgeon General has his or her own ideas of problems that deserve the highest priority. In the case of Dr. Antonia C. Novello, she targeted four areas as the cornerstones of her agenda: alcohol consumption, AIDS, smoking, and violence. Dr. Antonia C. Novello has crossed the country carrying her message.

Statistics of the Department of Justice show that nearly forty percent of young people in adult correctional facilities reported drinking before committing a crime, she has pointed out.

Novello believes storekeepers and law enforcement officials should be more vigilant and not allow drinking among the young. Parents should also be vigilant and set a good example. Surgeon General Novello has placed a great deal of the blame on alcohol-producing companies and their advertising agencies because they make drinking look glamorous. In this, as in other cases, she has named names, like Budweiser and Coors, something other Surgeon Generals never did.

The Surgeon General's office has no legislative power, but Dr. Novello's criticism has been noticed by anti-alcohol lobbyists. "It is time for Congress to require this industry to inform the public about the health and safety risks that can go along with drinking," said Christine Lubinsky, of the National Council on Alcoholism and Drug Dependence. Perhaps, something will be done in the near future.

About AIDS, and HIV, the virus that causes the disease, Dr. Novello said in California on April 21, 1992: "We must work to provide HIV prevention education immediately — and not in isolation, but as an integral element of a comprehensive health curriculum that also provides education about sexuality and drug abuse. A dialogue between young people and their parents is critical to such education, and all views should be acknowledged and accommodated."

Smoking has been an important issue for every Surgeon General since 1964, and Dr. Antonia C. Novello is no exception. Though in 1990, Dr. Sullivan, the Secretary of Health and Human Services, went after the R. J. Reynolds's "Uptown" brand because it "targeted blacks," no Surgeon General had named brand names until Dr. Novello did so. She blamed the Phillip Morris company for aggressively promoting Virginia Slims cigarettes to women for years. "It is tragic and frightening that lung cancer has surpassed breast cancer as the number one cause of death in women," she said.

In an interview with *Safety & Health* magazine, Dr. Novello expanded on the cigarette theme: "I am deeply concerned about our new generation of smokers. More than 3,000 teenagers begin to smoke each day. In fact, if the current smoking rate among adults continues at its present level, at least 5 million of the 20 million children who now live in the United States will die of smoke-related diseases."

Of her fourth cornerstone, violence, Dr. Novello said in her California speech: "Violence is a major public health problem in America, and has an enormous impact on our nation as a whole. *Violence takes the lives of 50,000 persons each year*. For the United States as a whole, the homicide rate was 9 per 100,000 in 1988. For African-American youth, however, *homicide was the leading cause of death*. The homicide rate was more

than nine times the rate for white youth and *17
to 238 times the rate for all young men in Western
Europe.* Although violence affects all communities, it affects low income, minority, and the dis-
advantaged communities at much higher rates
than the general population."

Dr. Antonia C. Novello is a woman of infinite
compassion and infinite strength. In her office,
she surrounds herself with stuffed toys and children's drawings. She goes to hospitals and dis-
penses hugs and kisses to sick children. "Before
you are a doctor, you are a human being," she
says. "I know what it is to be confined to a bed,
hurting, and frightened."

Dr. Antonia C. Novello also tells anyone who
will listen that she has "no patience" for anyone
who uses an illness or disability as an excuse. "If
I could overcome an illness and accomplish what
I have accomplished, others can do it, too."

The Novellos have no children, but the Surgeon
General considers all the children in the country
her children. She personally started a massive
immunization program against measles in Puerto
Rico. The program, no doubt, will be continued
in other parts of the country.

Dr. Novello's term as Surgeon General ended
in 1993 with the inauguration of President Clinton, but she continues to speak out about the
health issues important to her. During her term
she made a difference, satisfying her wish that
"all the trips, all the speeches, all the chicken

dinners will have been worth it." She hopes her example will inspire minority children to study and work hard because in this country, "you can succeed." "Look at me, a poor girl from Fajardo!" she exclaims.

7
Franklin R. Chang-Díaz

The National Aeronautics and Space Administration called Dr. Franklin Ramón Chang-Díaz at the Charles Stark Draper Laboratory in Cambridge, Massachusetts, one day in May 1980. The call was unexpected and when he answered the phone, Dr. Chang-Díaz was not in his own office at the lab but in another office across the street. He was told that he had been selected to be an astronaut and if he wanted to work for the agency and fly in space he had to go to the Johnson Space Center in Houston, Texas, for training.

"When I went back to the lab, I was so excited . . . it was as if I already were in space . . . I had to cross a well-traveled street and started crossing without looking," Dr. Chang-Díaz recalls. "I was almost killed! What I had dreamed of all those years almost didn't happen."

That might have been the only time emotion overtook this man so completely — but it happened before he became an astronaut. Astronauts must always have their emotions under control, have "nerves of steel," as it is often said. Franklin Chang-Díaz has demonstrated time and again that he has what it takes to be an astronaut.

When Franklin Chang-Díaz was seven years old, and living in San Juan de los Morros, Venezuela, he was quite interested in observing the stars in the deep blue sky. That year, the then-Soviet Union, which included Russia, launched the first satellite into space, *Sputnik I*. Newspapers and radio stations throughout the world carried the news.

"The year 1957 was a key year, an important year for me — maybe for many people," says Chang-Díaz. "I was fascinated by the idea that a machine made by human beings was now a new 'star' in the sky. I remember my mother telling me that if I looked hard after sunset I might get to see that little 'star.' I used to go to a park near our house, climb up a mango tree, and try to find it."

The seven-year-old never saw *Sputnik I* from his perch but the boy fell in love with outer space. That love was so great that it has remained with the man all his life.

Franklin Ramón Chang-Díaz was born in San José, Costa Rica, on April 5, 1950. His parents, Ramón A. Chang-Morales and María Eugenia Díaz de Chang, had six children, three girls and

three boys; Franklin was the second child, the oldest of the boys. His paternal grandfather was born in China, the rest of his immediate ancestors, in Costa Rica.

His parents were poor and didn't have much schooling, but Ramón Chang-Morales was filled with the spirit of adventure. So he headed for Venezuela with his family when the oil boom in that South American country required extra workers. Mr. Chang-Morales easily found employment with the Ministry of Public Works as a foreman on a construction crew.

"There were no astronauts then," says Chang-Díaz, "but I read a lot of science fiction, Jules Verne's stories, for example, and other stories about space conquests. I made up my mind then that I would become a 'space explorer,' my concept of what later became an 'astronaut.'

"All of this was before there were manned spacecrafts, before the Russians sent a little dog named Laika into space."

The so-called space race between the Soviet Union and the United States had started. The Soviet Union selected its first cosmonauts. The United States selected seven men to be its first astronauts.

Chang-Díaz continues his reminiscences during an interview. "Then came another important event — the first man went into space, [Soviet cosmonaut] Yuri Gagarin. I believe it was in 1961. We had returned to Costa Rica and I was going to school, with the idea [of flying in space] always in my mind. In those days I didn't know any English. I remember clipping every article [about space] I found in newspapers and magazines . . . gathering information."

By age ten or eleven, he was playing astronaut, lying on his back in a large cardboard box equipped with parts of old radios and TV sets, trying to simulate being in a space capsule. "My friends and I used to get inside this makeshift spaceship. We would go to a countdown, a liftoff, and we would go off and explore make-believe new planets," he says.

In his high school yearbook, there's a picture of Chang-Díaz and a friend in their multistage rocket, designed for the school science fair. While his friends also played space explorer and designed spacecrafts for the science fair, they followed different paths and careers when they grew up. Only Chang-Díaz became an astronaut.

When Chang-Díaz finished in La Salle, a parochial high school in San José, Costa Rica (1967), he tells us, "I started making plans to realize my dream. That's when I wrote to NASA, to the famous scientist Werner von Braun, the father of modern rocketry." He wrote asking how to become an astronaut.

"I received an answer from NASA," the astronaut says. "It was a form letter, nothing personalized, but at least I made contact." It has been reported that the answer said you should study science if you want to become an astronaut.

Now it was time to put the plan into action. "I

decided to leave Costa Rica and go to the United States and find the way to embark on this adventure," says Chang-Díaz. "I didn't know, really, how I was going to do it, but I knew I wanted a career in science. That was very clear in my mind, that in order to be an astronaut I should first be a scientist."

Methodically, like the good scientist he would become, Franklin Chang-Díaz started working on his plan. "As soon as I graduated from high school, I took a job in a bank, the Banco Nacional de Costa Rica, in order to save money for my trip," he says. "I couldn't save too much because, to tell you the truth, salaries weren't very high."

Nine or ten months later, with his entire savings of $50 and a one-way ticket, young Chang-Díaz took a flight to the United States. Ramón Chang-Morales, the family adventurer, "a man so full of self-confidence that he could do anything," bought the ticket for his son.

Lino and Betty Zúñiga and their children, distant relatives of the Chang-Díaz family, were then living in Hartford, Connecticut. Franklin Chang-Díaz had contacted them from Costa Rica and they readily welcomed him into their home. "I owe them a lot; they were the ones who helped me with my first steps in this country," he says. "They were very hard-working people but with a very low income, and there were ten of them, now eleven."

When he first arrived, there were a few important things to do. "I thought that to find my way in this society I had to learn English," says Chang-Díaz. "Second, I had to prepare for winter, which was coming. I had never seen snow. I only had my clothes from Costa Rica, so I spent 35 of my 50 dollars on a coat." With the help of Mr. and Mrs. Zúñiga, Chang-Díaz enrolled as a senior-year student at Hartford High School. This, he thought, could lead him to learning English and to a scholarship.

In high school, Franklin Chang-Díaz knew and understood very little of his new language and was sent to a special class to learn English. "Only the teacher spoke English in that class, I talked to the other kids in Spanish all the time," he says. He began to fail so he begged the principal and the counselor to send him to the regular classes. The young student persuaded them, after much reluctance on their part, to let him try.

For a while, Franklin Chang-Díaz continued to get very poor grades because he didn't understand or converse easily in English. But after about three months, he was able to communicate in this new language and by the end of the school year, he was in the top portion of his class. The boy no longer felt as homesick and lonely as he had felt on his first Christmas away, when he wanted to return to Costa Rica.

NASA's space program was now in full swing. President John F. Kennedy had declared that the United States would put a man on the moon before the end of the 1960s. In fact, U.S. astronauts walked on the moon in 1969, the same year the young Costa Rican dreamer graduated from a U.S. high school. "I remember exactly where I was when those men landed on the moon. I remember getting chills and telling myself that one day I'd be doing something like that," says Chang-Díaz.

School officials were very impressed with the future astronaut's progress. They recommended him for a scholarship given by the State of Connecticut. "It wasn't necessarily the grades that interested them, it was my effort and change, from the very bottom to very high," he says. A scholarship was granted for Chang-Díaz to attend the University of Connecticut.

"When I went to register at the University of Connecticut," says the astronaut, "they told me they were very sorry but they couldn't accept me. I couldn't have the scholarship because an error had been made, they said. They thought I was from Puerto Rico instead of Costa Rica. A Puerto Rican is a U.S. citizen; a Costa Rican is not."

State scholarships are to be granted to U.S. citizens or permanent residents in the United States. Franklin Chang-Díaz hadn't known that requirement at the time. He was neither a citizen nor a permanent resident — he had only a temporary tourist visa.

The news was a shock because he had been accepted by several other universities but had already told them he was going to the University of Connecticut. Now he had no money, no job, no scholarship, no admission. Franklin Chang-Díaz didn't panic, however, and went to discuss the matter with school officials.

The school officials were moved by Chang-Díaz's plight and went to the state legislature to try to change the law. The legislature met in an extraordinary session, made an exception, and granted the Costa Rican a one-year scholarship, "to rectify the error." "That's one of the nicest things that ever happened to me in this country," says the astronaut today. "For me, that's the United States of America, where the concept of fairness is very important."

With that hurdle out of the way, Chang-Díaz changed his tourist visa to a foreign student visa, which made it possible for him to work legally in certain jobs related to his studies. He immediately found a position in a physics lab at the university, a post he kept during his four years at the school.

When classes were in session, Chang-Díaz worked part time. During summer vacations, and between sessions, he worked full time. Thus he was able to leave the Zúñigas and provide for himself. He decided to be on his own not because the Zúñigas didn't want him living with them, but because he felt that one more person to feed was an additional burden for the family.

In the 1970s, after the moon landings, interest in the space program decreased in the United States. NASA's budget was cut and aerospace engineers were laid off. But for Franklin Chang-Díaz, the dream was still very much alive. "I used to tell people I was studying to be an astronaut, and everybody told me I was a little crazy," he recalls with a chuckle.

"At first I thought of studying aerospace engineering," he says, "but then I thought I wanted to be more than a conventional aerospace engineer, I wanted to be a rocket inventor — something like my great idol, Dr. von Braun — and go to other planets. That's why I studied mechanical engineering."

In four years time, Franklin Chang-Díaz received a bachelor of science degree with a double major in physics and mechanical engineering. In 1973, he went on to graduate school, at the Massachusetts Institute of Technology (MIT) in Cambridge, Massachusetts. Chang-Díaz became involved with a project he calls very "futuristic" in which people from many countries were involved. It was called *controlled thermonuclear fusion*. That's the same process used in the hydrogen bomb, he explains, but in a controlled manner, to produce electricity.

"This was almost like the science fiction I had read as a child, and it fascinated me," the scientist says. "I figured that in the future, spaceships would use that type of energy to move about in space. I could see a close connection between this [project] and the space program."

Chang-Díaz studied plasma physics, the area in which controlled thermonuclear fusion belongs, and graduated with a Ph.D. from MIT in 1977.

As luck would have it, in 1977 the Charles Stark Draper Laboratory, "around the corner from MIT," had a job opening for a mechanical engineer-scientist. That lab had designed all the navigational and control systems used in NASA's *Apollo* program, the spaceships that had gone to the moon. Draper needed someone to design control systems for atomic fusion reactors. The job had nothing to do with the space program but it was the same type of work, and Dr. Chang-Díaz, having the right qualifications, was hired.

As soon as his work started at Draper, Chang-Díaz learned that the space shuttle had been built and NASA was beginning to test it. "The idea of becoming an astronaut, which had sort of receded in my mind — because the space program was somewhat dormant — awakened," he says. "NASA began soliciting applicants in 1977, and my 'light bulb' was turned on!"

At this time, Chang-Díaz was going through the process of becoming a U.S. citizen. Most of the paperwork was done by then, but the whole process takes several years. No matter, Chang-Díaz prepared the paperwork to apply to become an astronaut.

The future astronaut was not accepted the first time. "I have never been told why, but I have the feeling it was because my [U.S.] citizenship had not been granted yet," he says. "I decided I would not give up after just one try — I had worked so hard towards my goal — so I said to myself, 'I'll stay here [at the lab] and get some more experience, and there will be another opportunity.' "

Teresa Gómez, chief assistant at NASA's Astronaut Selection Office, recently told an interviewer, "About 10 percent [of the applicants] are
disqualified immediately because they don't
meet the qualifications — they aren't U.S. citizens, or they don't have a degree in science or
engineering."

In 1979, when NASA solicited applicants again,
Chang-Díaz took out his papers from his file, up-
dated his résumé, and applied again. By now he
was a U.S. citizen.

Several months later, a letter and a phone call
from NASA invited Chang-Díaz to go to the Johnson Space Center for preliminary interviews and
tests. He had passed the preselection process and
was to spend one week in Houston.

"I met lots of men and women who wanted to
be astronauts, everyone an adventurer and vi-
sionary, everyone a highly qualified scientist,"
Chang-Díaz says. "For the first time I could see
myself reflected in those people. But I was the
only Latin, the only Spanish-speaking person
born in another country."

Other astronauts have been born in different
countries, but their parents were U.S. citizens.
Two other Hispanics were in space before Chang-
Díaz: Arnaldo Tamayo Méndez, from Cuba, in a
Soviet mission; and Rodolfo Neri Vela, from Mex-
ico, in the American mission just before Chang-
Díaz's first mission. However, both these men
were on a special one-time assignment. Franklin

R. Chang-Díaz is the first Hispanic to be in the space program for the long run.

After the tests, Chang-Díaz went home. Many months passed without news from Houston. At last, in 1980, came that exciting, hoped-for call. From hundreds and hundreds of highly qualified applicants, only nineteen had been selected. Chang-Díaz called his parents in Costa Rica as soon as he got to his desk. "My father cried," he says, "the emotion was too much for him. I had worked so hard for this. He was so happy for me."

Dr. Franklin Chang-Díaz moved to Houston, Texas, in 1980, and became an astronaut in training. He still lives in Houston, with his second wife, the former Peggy Margaret Doncaster, and his three daughters, Jean, Sonia, and Lidia.

He was officially named an astronaut in August 1981. This is how NASA documents describe his activities:

While in training, he was also involved in flight software checkout at the Shuttle Avionics Integration Laboratory (SAIL), and participated in the early space station design studies. In late 1982, he was designated as support crew for the first Spacelab mission and, in November 1983, served as an orbit capsule communicator (CAPCOM) during that flight.

From October 1984 to August 1985, he was leader of the astronaut support team at the Kennedy Space Center. His duties included astronaut support during the processing of the various vehicles and pay-

loads, as well as flight crew support during the final
phases of the launch countdown.

STS 61-C, the official designation of Chang-
Díaz's first mission, was scheduled for launching
at the end of 1985 but, for a variety of reasons, it
was postponed seven times.

At long last, the big day for Chang-Díaz dawned
at the launching site at Kennedy Space Center,
Florida, on January 12, 1986. The flight marked
the return to service of the Shuttle *Columbia*,
which had been undergoing renovation since
1983.

As that spaceship finally took off, in one of the
most flawless launches NASA has ever had,
Franklin Chang-Díaz's lifelong quest was no
longer a dream. "When I was strapped in that
spaceship ready for liftoff, all I could think about
was my childhood games in a cardboard box,"
the astronaut says. "It seemed incredible that this
was for real."

Unfortunately, Mr. Chang-Morales, the astronaut's hero, did not live long enough to see his
son actually launched into space, but he did see
him in training.

During this flight, Dr. Chang-Díaz helped
launch the SATCOM-KU satellite, operated a lab,
and conducted various experiments in astro-
physics. He also videotaped a guided tour of the
shuttle in Spanish, for broadcast to Latin America and the United States. It was one way of telling everyone that dreams do come true.

On the tour, Chang-Díaz showed his fellow astronauts at work and explained what each was doing. He demonstrated how astronauts sleep and how they move about inside the spacecraft. He showed some of the experiments he was conducting. He also showed a beautiful view of the earth from the shuttle's window.

After viewing the broadcast beamed from space, the President of Costa Rica placed an earth-to-space phone call to the astronauts. The president told Chang-Díaz of the excitement felt in the entire country of Costa Rica.

Even in the most remote areas the events were being followed. The president asked Chang-Díaz a question that a peasant wanted answered: "What did the astronauts eat?" Chang-Díaz explained that in space the astronauts ate a lot of what they ate at home, and he showed a package of tortillas. NASA had made sure the people in Costa Rica could see the astronauts on TV when the conversation was taking place.

Following ninety-six orbits' of the earth, the mission ended in a perfect night landing at Edwards Air Force Base, California, on January 18 — 146 hours, 3 minutes, and 51 seconds after liftoff. Those were great moments for Chang-Díaz.

Chang-Díaz has said that the general public doesn't know enough about the space program. When the program first started, people followed the news, but after a while they stopped paying attention. Chang-Díaz once told *The Christian Science Monitor*, "John Glenn orbited the earth

three times. Jack Lousma was in space for three
months, but nobody knows him."

It was because Chang-Díaz felt that the public
was not well informed that he decided to make
the video in space. He told *Nuestro* magazine, "I
have always found that there's a great lack of
information on matters pertaining to the activities on board the space shuttle. We hear a little
about, yes, the space shuttle went up, but then
there's not a whole lot of substance to it.

"What I wanted to add was perhaps a little
more substance for Latin America and also for
Spanish-speaking people in this country as to
what's going on in the space shuttle and how this
sort of activity can benefit them so immensely."

On October 18, 1989, Chang-Díaz went into
space for the second time on Space Shuttle *Atlantis*. During this flight, the *Galileo* spacecraft
was sent out to explore the planet Jupiter. The
crew also mapped atmospheric ozone, conducted
experiments involving radiation measurements,
and did research on lightning. One of Chang-
Díaz's experiments involved determining the direction corn and other plant roots grow in the
absence of gravity. After seventy-nine orbits of
the earth, the mission ended on October 23 at
Edwards Air Force Base — 119 hours and 41 minutes after liftoff.

Chang-Díaz's third mission was also aboard
Space Shuttle *Atlantis*, which lifted off on July
31, 1992. The European Retrievable Carrier
(EURECA) was launched from this flight, and the

first Tethered Satellite System (TSS) was conducted. The mission completed 126 orbits of the earth in 3.35 million miles — 191 hours, 16 minutes, and 7 seconds after liftoff.

As of December 1992, Chang-Díaz had logged over 1,500 hours of flight time, including 1,300 hours in jet aircraft. He had also logged 457 hours in space.

To prepare for his fourth mission, Chang-Díaz trained in Russia as well as the United States. This flight of the shuttle *Discovery*, a purely scientific mission originally scheduled for November 1993, lifted off from the Kennedy Space Center on February 3, 1994. Landing was at the same site eight days later, on February 11, after circling the earth 131 times and traveling 3,439,704 miles. Though astronauts and cosmonauts shook hands in space in 1975, when the American *Apollo* and the Soviet *Soyuz* linked up for a while, this 1994 flight was historic because a Russian cosmonaut flew in an American craft for the first time.

There were difficulties with certain parts of the mission, and a satellite that might yield information to make faster computers was not deployed. But, as reported in *The New York Times*, all the while, "the payload commander, Dr. Franklin R. Chang-Díaz, tended science experiments in a commercial laboratory called Spacehab riding in the cargo bay." Twelve of the thirteen Spacehab experiments — dealing with microgravity, heat dissipation in space, developing new pharmaceutical products, and testing new agricultural technology — were successful. Tests results and observations of the earth will be shared by the United States and Russia.

Chang-Díaz didn't set out to be the first Hispanic in the space program — he just wanted to be an astronaut. But he is aware that circumstances have made him a role model. Whatever he does reflects on his fellow Hispanics and can even influence them.

His example rubbed off on his own mother: María Eugenia Díaz de Chang finished high school at age fifty-four, after her son was already an astronaut, and immediately went to college. "My mother has become a sort of celebrity in Costa Rica," Chang-Díaz says proudly. "She now spends a lot of her time giving talks in schools and other gatherings."

Whenever his schedule allows it, Chang-Díaz talks before school groups and other audiences, in the United States as well as throughout Latin America. "It is an honor to be a representative of a group increasingly becoming powerful in the U.S.," he once said. "But I hope we'll grow out into society and not have to pay attention to race or color. In the meantime, I know it's important to have role models."

A high school junior, himself thinking of an engineering career, heard Chang-Díaz that day and responded, "The reality that he's a Hispanic astronaut kind of makes you feel important . . . like if he can do it, anyone can do it."

"Nowadays, I receive hundreds of letters from

children — they come from all over Latin America and the United States," says Chang-Díaz. "When I read the letters, I think of myself writing to NASA, and I hope that at least one of those children will become an astronaut."

Since NASA has no age limit for retirement and Franklin Chang-Díaz is thoroughly happy with his job, he plans to remain an astronaut as long as he is physically fit. Nowadays, he is thinking about Mars because "that's where the future is." He'd love to spend some time on Mars — perhaps aboard a space vehicle he'd help to design and develop!

8
Fernando Bujones

One day in July 1974, a tired nineteen-year-old was taking a nap in Varna, Bulgaria. He had just danced in the Varna International Ballet Competition, considered the Olympics of the ballet world. María Calleiro woke up her sleeping son with a kiss.

"The results are in," the mother said. He sprang up and asked her, "Did I win?" "You won a bronze medal," she said. "Bronze? Is that all?" the son said, trying to hide his disappointment. "I'm just teasing you," the mother said. "You won the gold medal, the first prize, and also a special certificate for the highest technical achievement."

María Calleiro's son jumped for joy — and well he should, for he is Fernando Bujones, known for jumps and leaps very few male ballet dancers have ever been able to achieve.

Fernando Bujones had become a professional dancer only a short time earlier; now he became the first American-born male ballet dancer to win the gold.

More than twenty years after his professional debut, Bujones is still dancing, shining brightly on stages all over the world, showing why he won that first prize.

Fernando Bujones was born in Miami, Florida, on March 9, 1955. His father, Fernando Bujones, Sr., as well as his mother, María Calleiro, were born in Cuba. He is their only child, though the elder Bujones has another son and two daughters by a second marriage.

When Bujones was a child, work opportunities made his family move about between Cuba and the United States. During one of the periods living in Cuba, five-year-old Fernando would not eat. "I'm just not hungry," the boy would say at mealtime. His mother worried he might be ill and took him to the doctor.

"The doctor said there was nothing wrong with me, that I just wanted attention," he recalls. His mother talked to friends and relatives about this situation, and someone suggested that exercise might improve the boy's appetite.

María Calleiro thought about it and then came up with a wonderful idea. She had always been interested in the arts, having studied ballet with Fernando Alonso in Havana, Cuba, as well as being an actress on the stage. (She now writes poetry and short stories.) She thought that ballet lessons would give her son exercise and introduce him to the arts at the same time.

So it was that Fernando Bujones took his first ballet lessons in Havana as a little boy. He took classes in two government-run schools. "I loved ballet right away," he says. He could jump and leap all he wanted, he was in the company of other kids, and his teachers paid attention to his every move.

Without knowing it, Fernando Bujones had found his calling. He had started a life that requires great self-discipline and long hours of practice and rehearsals day after day after day.

By the time Bujones was about nine and a half years old, politics and life had changed dramatically in Cuba. Fidel Castro's revolutionary regime had taken hold. The United States had broken off relations with Cuba. People were restricted in many ways; they could no longer travel when and where they wanted to.

When the government did allow people to leave the country, they could not go directly to the United States. Young Fernando and his mother were able to obtain permission to leave, but to return to Florida they had to go by way of France.

When they arrived in Miami in 1964, they met relatives who had left Cuba earlier. One of those relatives was Bujones's cousin, Zeida Cecilia Méndez, a ballet dancer, who was now dancing with Ballet Concierto, a small company in Miami.

Fernando Bujones went to school in Miami but did not take any ballet lessons for about a year

and a half. "It was the trauma of being uprooted," he now explains.

Then Ballet Concierto needed a boy to dance the little prince in the *Nutcracker* ballet and Fernando was given the part. He resumed his ballet lessons twice a week and acquired a private coach, his cousin Zeida Cecilia Méndez, who would become a major influence in Bujones's life. He began dancing in ballets that call for boys, like *Peter and the Wolf*, when they made school presentations.

In 1966, Ballet Spectacular, a touring company composed of ballet dancers from all over the United States, danced in Miami. The featured lead dancers were Jacques D'Amboise and Melissa Hayden, stars of the New York City Ballet.

María Calleiro was working at this time as the stage manager in the theater where they performed, and she arranged an audition with D'Amboise for her young son.

Fernando Bujones danced for half an hour and Jacques D'Amboise liked what he saw. D'Amboise got Bujones a summer scholarship to attend the School of American Ballet in New York City.

Dance critic Iris M. Fanger says that the boy was "recognized as a prodigy by the age of twelve, when he arrived in New York City in the summer of 1967," and the School of American Ballet offered Fernando Bujones a full scholarship for the entire year.

Fernando's mother said he was too young to be on his own in the city and she would need some means of support in order to stay with him. The school secured a Ford Foundation grant for the son and paid a salary to the mother so she could take care of him. "They were *that* interested in my development," Bujones says now.

Fernando Bujones attended the School of American Ballet for five years, and took piano lessons in addition to ballet. He also attended the Professional Children's School to complete his academic studies.

Dance critic Patricia Barnes recalls those days vividly.

There was a young dancer in the class, she writes, *recently arrived from Miami, who showed unusual talent. The dancer was Fernando Bujones, at twelve years old, still with the frame of a boy, but with the manner, concentration, and persistence of an experienced professional.*

I watched this child — for child he still clearly was — mesmerized. Never before had I seen such devotion, or such remarkable physical form at such an early age. Already there was body line, style, musicality, and most evidently, a burgeoning virtuoso technique.

At the age of fourteen, Fernando Bujones, still in school, received his first professional offer. "George Balanchine invited me to join his company, the New York City Ballet, but I thought I was still too young and didn't accept the offer," Bujones says. During his years in school, he danced many principal parts in school presentations of ballets like *La Sylphide*, *Coppelia*, and *Swan Lake*.

Bujones made his professional debut with the company of one of his teachers, the Eglevsky Ballet, in Massapequa Park, New York. In his first paid performance he danced the *pas de deux* from the ballet *Don Quixote* with Gelsey Kirkland. Seventeen-year-old Kirkland was already dancing professionally with the New York City Ballet, while fifteen-year-old Bujones was still in school. Patricia Barnes, who has followed his career intently, says that "he displayed the type of charisma in a personality, that comes only once or twice in a generation."

At age sixteen, Bujones was invited to dance with Ballet Spectacular, the same company that had brought D'Amboise to Miami a few years earlier. In this tour, the featured guest star was the legendary ballerina Margot Fonteyn, of the Royal Ballet.

With Ballet Spectacular, Bujones danced in Miami and other U.S. cities, as well as internationally — in Caracas, Venezuela; Managua, Nicaragua; and San José, Costa Rica, among others.

At age seventeen, Bujones received three important professional offers. Balanchine asked him again to join his New York City Ballet; Celia Franca asked him to dance the part of the bluebird in a production of *The Sleeping Beauty*, which Rudolf Nureyev was working on for her company, the National Ballet of Canada; and Lucia Chase asked him to join the American Ballet Theater, which she directed, in New York City.

In the end, Bujones chose the American Ballet Theater. Though he admired Balanchine's work, and very much would have liked to dance for Nureyev, the repertoire of American Ballet Theater was closer to the strictly classical ballets that had captivated him as a child.

Bujones had seen the Ballet Nacional de Cuba productions of *Coppelia*, *Giselle*, and *Swan Lake*, staged by the great Alicia Alonso. "My soul, my spirit, my enthusiasm was geared to the classics, not to abstract ballets. I admired and still admire Balanchine's choreography, but I thought that if I danced the classic ballets first, I could dance the others later," says Bujones about his decision.

Six months after joining the corps de ballet at American Ballet Theater, Bujones was promoted to principal male dancer, making him one of the youngest principal dancers in the world. He danced *Variations for Four* alongside already established principal male dancers.

Two or three months after becoming a principal dancer, Bujones went on his first tour with his company. While on tour, one of the other principal dancers, Ted Kivit, became injured, and his partner, Eleanor D'Antuono, requested that Bujones take his place.

In spite of the fact that American Ballet Theater was very conscious of seniority, and there were other male principal dancers available, Bujones got to partner the ballerina in the *Don Quixote* ballet. That was in 1973. That year he also danced before Princess Margaret and other members of the British royal family in a gala performance at the London Palladium.

The following year, Bujones traveled to Varna for the competition in which he won first prize. Being nineteen years old, he was still entitled to compete in the junior division, but he chose to compete in the senior division, with dancers as old as twenty-eight.

"It was a glorious moment," he fondly recalls. "There must have been 150 contestants, men and women." Bujones was the youngest male dancer in the adult competition, among dancers from all over the world, including the famous Bolshoi Ballet of the then-Soviet Union.

But the timing of this "glorious moment" and triumph was not exactly right. Bujones's return to the United States coincided with the defection of the Soviet ballet star Mikhail Baryshnikov. For the media in the United States, this defection was more than artistic news, it was a major political coup since the United States and the Soviet Union were engaged in the cold war.

The bulk of the headlines and stories was about the defector, not about the native son who had brought home such a great honor. "What could have been the great news," Bujones later said, "turned into a small eclipse."

Whenever he had the opportunity, Bujones said plainly and pointedly that he was being overlooked — and his frankness did not win him many friends among the dance critics. They called him arrogant, among other things. Audiences, however, have always been friendly to Bujones, wherever he has danced. Ballet audiences in New York City are special, he says. "Every artist should have the opportunity to perform in New York City."

Even to this day, Bujones will say, if asked, that recognition has been given to him more readily and freely in every other country than in his own. "I always remember that 'Nadie es profeta en su tierra,' " he says. Literally translated, the saying would be, "Nobody is a prophet in his own land."

According to Bujones, the minute there was a Russian or French dancer, or a dancer from any other European country, they would write more about the newcomer than about Bujones, the boy next door, so to speak. "But I have always liked a challenge," he says.

In 1976, while performing with the Rio de Janeiro Ballet, Bujones met and fell in love with Marcia Kubitscheck. The daughter of the former president of Brazil, Juscelino Kubitscheck, she was an associate director of the Rio de Janeiro Ballet at the time.

Marcia Kubitscheck and Fernando Bujones married in 1980 and have a daughter, Alejandra. Their home base was New York City. Though they were divorced in 1987, they maintain cordial relations. Bujones considers his years with Kubit-

scheck a very special time in his life. "For me, it
was a period of growth, artistically, personally,
and socially."

Alejandra now lives with her mother in Brazil,
but comes to visit her father in the United States
every year, and her father visits her twice a year
in Brazil. "She's very musical," Bujones says of
Alejandra. "I hope she follows a career in music."

Baryshnikov joined American Ballet Theater
and later succeeded Lucia Chase as director. Bujones remained with the company, though not
always happy, until 1985. He resigned that year
and went to Rio de Janeiro where he became assistant director of his wife's old ballet company.

Brazil was going through tough economic
times and the arts were not a top priority. "It was
very difficult for me to adapt," Bujones says. "I
was thirty years old and had to make a career
decision." He became a globe-trotting freelance
dancer whom many international dance companies in Europe, Asia, and North and South
America were eager to hire.

In 1986, while dancing in Denmark, he met
Bruce Marks, director of the Boston Ballet. Marks
offered Bujones a permanent position with his
company, a position Bujones accepted on condition he be given "permanent guest status" and
be allowed to tour. Bujones did not want to be
involved in the politics and problems of a company, he said.

Marks agreed to the star's requests, and since
1987 Bujones has had the best of both worlds:

a home base in Boston and the freedom to perform elsewhere whenever he wants. He has even returned to his old company, American Ballet Theater.

During guest appearances in Germany, in 1989, Bujones met Peruvian-born ballerina María Arnillas, then with the Stuttgart Ballet. "I was enchanted with her right away," he says. "At that moment in my life I needed a person like her, a Latin, who could understand me the way I am, who could be the perfect companion in every sense of the word."

Within a year, María Arnillas joined the Boston Ballet, and in 1991 Arnillas and Bujones married. "Marrying her is the best thing I could have done," he says.

The roster of dancers he has partnered during his meteoric and remarkable career includes, in Bujones's own words, "some of the most exquisite ballerinas of the twentieth century."

Throughout the years, many things have been written about Bujones. In 1981, Anna Kisselgoff wrote of him in *The New York Times, Could any dancer ever have jumped so high? It is the kind of feat one reads about but never sees and one that has, one suspects, never really been seen before.*

In 1986, Clement Crisp wrote about Bujones in Britain's *Financial Times, His aristocratic utterance — steps cut with purity and joyous energy; the dance — large in scale, beautiful in outline — is marvelous to behold. Each phrase, each position, has that rarest of qualities, true classic distinction.*

Patricia Barnes, in personal notes, wrote in 1991, *By instinct, he interprets with a Spanish fire and temperament that gives such individuality to his artistic profile in roles like Basil in* Don Quixote, *or the butler in* Miss Julie, *where Bujones unerringly captured the sensual complex nature of his character.*

Among the many honors that have come his way, Bujones has been named one of the Outstanding Young Men of America by the Library of Congress. He has received the *Dance Magazine* Award and *The New York Times* Award as the 1986 outstanding artistic talent from the State of Florida, as well as the Hispanic Heritage Award for Performing Arts from the Organization of American States.

In 1986, Bujones made a command performance for President Ronald Reagan at the White House. In 1987 he was invited by Yuri Grigorovich, the artistic director of the Bolshoi Ballet, to perform with his company in Russia. The same year, Maurice Béjart created *Trois Etudes pour Alexandre*, a ballet based on Alexander the Great, especially for Bujones.

In 1990, the Boston Ballet did an experiment that *Newsweek* magazine called "a *'Swan Lake'* made in heaven." Dancers from Russia and from the United States danced together on the same stage. Bolshoi's Nina Ananiashvili danced the dual role of Odette/Odile, the white/black swan, and Boston's Fernando Bujones partnered her as the Prince.

The following year, the governor of the state of Massachusetts issued a special proclamation in honor of Bujones's twentieth year of dancing. The Boston Ballet had a special gala performance in May for this anniversary. His American Ballet Theater long-time partner, Cynthia Gregory, went to Boston to dance with him.

Dance critic Christine Temin covered the event for the *Boston Globe* and wrote, *Then, at the very end, he stood all alone under the chandeliers, playing the role that has seemed to come so naturally to him for the last two decades: the Prince.*

Though he has been on stage for more than twenty years, dance critics state that his prodigious technical skills and his highly charged performance qualities have not diminished. If anything, his years of experience have given his dancing a more well-rounded, polished quality.

Critics have written in recent years that Bujones is willing to "share the stage with younger dancers." "His concentration onstage is total," says Iris M. Fanger, "and he seems to be as concerned with presenting his partner as himself." One of those young partners, Jennifer Gelfand, herself being called a prodigy these days, has said of Bujones, "I can't think of anyone I'd rather dance with."

Bujones is not content with being only a highly acclaimed ballet star. There are other parts of his world still to be conquered. He has recently been choreographing and staging numerous works. "After having — allow me to say it — a beautiful career, my dream for the future is to be the artistic director of a company," says Bujones. "The most important thing in life is to have a goal. I want to pass along to a new generation all the tradition, all the knowledge, all the skills that I have acquired throughout the years."

The tradition, knowledge, and skills Bujones speaks about are represented in his eclectic repertoire, ranging from the strictly classic ballets to the theatrical and modern ones.

Reminiscing about his life and accomplishments, Fernando Bujones says he has been fortunate and is thankful to four women who have made a difference in his life. "I couldn't have done what I have done without them," says the star.

Those Bujones credits are his mother, a single parent who worked very hard to make sure he had what he needed when he needed it; his cousin, the coach who helped him develop to his full potential and "polished" his style; his first wife, who gave him strength; and his present wife, who gives him support and understanding.

"Since I was a child, I always wanted to excel," he says. "I remember asking my cousin and coach, 'What would happen if I couldn't get to be a soloist dancer?' And she said to me, 'That has to concern you more than anyone else,' I worried about letting down the people around me, the people who loved me."

No matter what she said to him, the coach knew that in her hands was a gem that one day would sparkle with a dazzling brilliance. She worked the future star very hard, but she also gave him confidence in his abilities.

Recently, Bujones wrote about his coach: "Sometimes Zeida would be so demanding that I would start thinking she could never be pleased, no matter what I did. But deep inside of me I knew that if she still asked for more, it was because she knew I could do better; not only better, she wanted me to be the best. And I loved being at my best."

Fernando Bujones has not let down his loved ones, nor his audiences. He is always at his best.

9
Miriam Santos

Once there was a girl from a *barrio* who sat uncomfortably in a speech therapy class in Gary, Indiana. From there, she traveled a long, narrow, winding road that led her to other schools and other neighborhoods. Some years passed, and now she is the grown woman who sits in the comfortable office of the city treasurer in Chicago.

The journey began on January 6, 1956, the day Miriam Santos was born to Ana and Manolín Santos. Her parents had come to industrial Indiana from Puerto Rico in search of a better life. Miriam is the second of five children, the first of two girls.

Neither Mr. Santos nor Mrs. Santos had the opportunity to get a good education. In Puerto Rico, Manolín Santos was able to complete the eighth grade, but Ana Santos could only finish the third. In Gary, Indiana, Mr. Santos was a

factory worker in a steel mill, where he became
active in the union; Mrs. Santos worked in various factory jobs. There they toiled until, eventually, both of them suffered industrial accidents
that disabled them, while their children were still
young. Today, Mr. Santos suffers from many ailments attributed to exposure to radiation. Mrs.
Santos's hands were maimed when they were
caught in a machine.

But what Mr. and Mrs. Santos lacked in formal
education and financial resources, they more
than made up for in love, reassurance, and encouragement for their children. Their adult children often travel to see them in Puerto Rico,
where they live in retirement, or bring them to
the mainland for family gatherings.

The Santos children went to school knowing
only Spanish. They had no speech impediments,
but they wound up in speech therapy class.
"That's where they sent all the 'Spanish' kids in
that school in those days, whether they belonged
there or not," Santos says. The Hispanic students
did not get much help from their teachers, but
some of them managed to learn nonetheless.

Miriam Santos recalls many humiliating situ-
ations from her childhood, as well as the way her
parents helped her maintain her self-esteem. One
incident Santos retells often is about the time
some kids called her a "spic," and when she complained, the teacher also used the same nasty
word. In tears, the little girl told her mother
about it.

"Honey," Mrs. Santos said, holding her daughter on her lap, soothing and comforting her, "you have to understand that you're a special child because you have two cultures and speak two languages. The teacher knows that but can't treat you any differently because she has so many other kids."

From then on, says Santos, "if anyone teased me about speaking Spanish, I'd say, 'That's okay. I'm special.' " And from then on, she has always tried to turn something negative into something positive.

Miriam Santos used to attend union rallies with her father, who "was very informed when it came to politics." She believes she became aware of politics and social problems way back then. By age ten, Miriam Santos was already a seasoned interpreter who accompanied her parents and other non-English-speaking adults to offices and places where only English was spoken. On one such occasion, the little girl interpreted for a middle-aged couple fighting a traffic ticket.

"I felt so badly for this poor couple," Santos recalls now, "just dealing with the clerk was so humiliating for them. He was abusive because they couldn't speak English, and then the judge was abusive to them, too. I could have died for them; it was so awful. I just thought, 'Don't yell at them, please. They shouldn't be subjected to this. They shouldn't be treated this way.' "

Santos saw her own parents and other Hispanics and blacks being treated disrespectfully, and

"I decided I wanted to be a lawyer and be able to help people."

The Santos children have worked since they were very young. At age twelve, Miriam Santos got a job as a part-time bookkeeper in a machine shop that was conveniently located on the ground floor of the building where her family lived. "Even then, I was good with numbers," Santos points out.

In high school, Santos did very well — she skipped a grade, and graduated with honors. The family then moved to Chicago, but hardship seemed to follow them. On the day of Miriam's seventeenth birthday, a fire ravaged their apartment and some of the children had to go back to Gary to stay with relatives. This was a very difficult time for such a close-knit family but they were able to recover soon thereafter and be together again.

In 1973, Miriam Santos became the first in her family to attend college when she entered DePaul University in Chicago. She had scholarships throughout her college years but continued working all the while to supplement her scholarship earnings and to help out at home. Part of the time, her work was the 3-to-11 P.M. shift in a factory.

One job Miriam Santos recalls all too well and not very fondly was assembling Christmas ornaments. She had to work so fast that sometimes her hands would get cut on the machinery. After bandaging her up, the boss would make her go back to work immediately. When scholarships and earnings weren't sufficient, she took out bank loans.

In 1977, Santos graduated with a Bachelor of Arts in Political Science, with honors, from DePaul University; in 1980, she received a law degree from DePaul University College of Law.

Even in her college and law school days, Miriam Santos found time for community service, sometimes on a volunteer basis, sometimes as an employee. She ran a legal clinic for Casa Central, a social service organization based in Chicago. She became a board member when that organization was creating a housing project for poor Hispanics.

Santos was also involved in the creation of a nursing home for the elderly — "a new concept for Hispanics," she says. "We don't usually put our people in nursing homes; the elderly live with someone, a relative."

After graduating from law school, Miriam Santos went to work in a small law firm in Chicago, for Robert Mann, her parents' attorney. "I liked him, he treated my parents with a lot of respect," she says, "and he was also heavily involved in a political campaign." It was at that time that Santos met Richard Daley, then running for state attorney.

About a year later, Santos got a job in Washington, D.C., as executive director for educational equity for ASPIRA, Inc. ASPIRA (Spanish for "to aspire") is a national nonprofit organization, founded in 1961, whose function is to encourage and promote education and develop leadership among young Hispanics.

On behalf of ASPIRA, Santos lobbied in Congress for educational opportunities for Hispanics. But this was in the early 1980s and, she says, "it was a really shocking time to be in Washington if you were on 'the wrong side' of the issues.'" In other words, "advocacy and social issues were not a prime concern for the government."

She went back to Illinois and joined the political campaign of Adlai Stevenson, who was running for governor. "Adlai Stevenson was wonderful. I began to reflect that there were *good* people who had good agendas in politics. That's how I *really* began my involvement with local politics," Miriam Santos admits.

With Stevenson's campaign over, Miriam Santos went to work for state attorney Richard Daley in 1983. Her job was that of deputy director and prosecutor of child support enforcement.

In the year that followed, Miriam Santos went to work in the public sector as an attorney for Illinois Bell Telephone Co. "I wanted to make some money, with school loans due . . . my parents were ill . . ." she explains. Soon she was promoted to division manager for customer and community relations.

Now Santos was making good money, and was able to afford better housing. However, she kept all her ties with the Hispanic community and got involved with other community organizations, such as the Mexican American Legal Defense and

Educational Fund (MALDEF), and the Hispanic Higher Education Coalition. "I did pro bono [free of charge] cases while I was at Illinois Bell. I represented the indigent on my own time."

In spite of this flurry of activity, Miriam Santos found the time to enroll in the Master of Business Administration program at Northwestern University in Chicago.

"Illinois Bell was a good company to work for," says Santos. Her superiors allowed and encouraged her to do exciting and worthwhile things. Once they "lent" her out for six months, as executive-on-loan to Chicago United, a group of leading black, white, and Hispanic executives representing major corporations, minority-owned business, and community organizations. Santos's responsibility was to make sure the programs met the needs of the Hispanic community.

In 1989, Richard Daley was elected mayor in a special election after his predecessor, Harold Washington, died in office. Daley called on Miriam Santos to be a member of his transition team, and soon offered her the job of city treasurer.

It was a hard decision for Santos — she had just gotten another promotion at Illinois Bell, with a salary increase to match. She "felt like Santa Claus," Santos says, because now she would be able to "contribute to all the causes and charities I could think of." At first she told the mayor, "No, I'm just doing what I want to do now. I am happy at Illinois Bell."

But Mayor Daley kept trying. Finally, the po-

tential for community development that she saw
in the city job won her over, and Miriam Santos
accepted the offer. As city treasurer, she manages
$60 billion annually.

Santos is the treasurer and manager of investment holdings for the Board of Education of the
city of Chicago, and for four city pension funds
— fire, police, labor, and municipal employees.
In addition, she is the custodian of the Teacher's
Pension Fund, the first female and first Hispanic
to hold that particular job.

In most cities, the office of the city treasurer
does not normally generate a lot of news. In Chicago, it does so "only at election time," one news-
paperman has said. But when Miriam Santos
took that post in Chicago, news began to come
out of the city treasurer's office almost every day.
News came at a fast and furious pace because
things turned around 180 degrees. Newspapers
and magazines as far away from Chicago as
Washington, D.C., Miami, Los Angeles, and Boston began writing stories about the new city
treasurer at work.

"My first day in the office, I found more than
one million dollars in cold cash in a safe in that
room." Santos points from her desk. "Imagine!"

When she asked why that money was kept
there, the new treasurer was told it was needed
to cash the paychecks of city employees. In an
office called "the cage," right next door to the
treasurer's office, the checks were cashed. "But
people get paid only twice a month," Santos says.

"Having one million dollars here every day didn't make any sense, and it increased the potential for theft!" So the money went to a bank where it earns interest for the city.

To solve the problem of employees who need to cash their paychecks and don't have a bank account, Santos contracted with a bank to provide the service. The bank, a private institution, was chosen by competitive bidding and the lowest bidder was Seaway National Bank, a minority-owned bank.

Now Seaway opens "the cage" in city hall at designated times and sells Chicago Transit Authority bus tokens and monthly passes to city employees. The city pays the bank for its services. Even so, it saves more than $475,000 a year by having a private bank, instead of city employees, do the job.

Innovation has followed innovation under Miriam Santos's direction. Employees who were not needed, or not productive enough, or were involved in dishonest deals, were let go. She had discovered a Manila envelope stuffed with $947 million in securities [bonds or certificates of stock] in a safe, "along with potato chips, soft drinks, and somebody's shoes," Santos told *The Miami Herald.*

All the changes were necessary because, in her words, she "had a staff that found ways to steal money, an accounting department without accountants or accountability." Miriam Santos hired fewer people, but with better educational

credentials, and paid them higher salaries. She
is comfortable with the staff she has now.

In 1990, Miriam Santos received her MBA degree from Northwestern University's Kellogg
School of Business, and continued changing
things at work. That year, she replaced the manual ledger system with sophisticated computer
equipment and software, a more efficient way to
keep track of the money and manage the city's
budget of $3.1 billion a year.

"For me, having good, solid information
means, for instance, that I know I have exactly
$87 million to invest today, so I can get bulk rate
prices and [use this to] compare rates," Santos
told *Computerworld.*

The new system also helped the treasurer track
a check-cashing scam that put her predecessor in
a bad light. Although her predecessor was a political friend of the mayor, Miriam Santos did not
cover up the scam.

Another brainchild of Santos's is a program
to provide loans to Chicago's small businesses.
Loans range from $5,000 to $50,000. The program
has been endorsed by the Federal Deposit Insur-
ance Corporation and the Federal Reserve Board,
the highest banking authorities in the country.
This loan program is important, Santos says, because "small businesses are the greatest source
of new employment in Chicago," and "a small
loan is often enough capital to support a company
through difficult times, and save jobs."

Meanwhile, the city treasurer's relations with

her political mentor, Mayor Richard Daley, were not good. She says people close to the mayor told her she was "rocking the boat," that she was too "independent." Many people in Chicago think that her "troubles" began when she exposed the check-cashing scam at a "politically wrong time," because her predecessor was running for state attorney.

In an extensive interview with *Today's Chicago Woman*, Santos explains why she took action when she did. "I had to choose between keeping something quiet because there was an election going on and doing the right thing.

"I didn't create the problem — I inherited those staff members who were guilty of embezzlement — but if I hadn't taken care of it after it came to my attention, it would've been my problem.

"I had to move this office beyond making decisions based on their political impact to making decisions based on what was in the best interests of the taxpayers."

Also by way of explanation, Santos says, "My first week here, $5,200 disappeared from the cashier's cage, and no one seemed to care. The attitude was, '5,200 bucks, so what?' All I could think was, Do you know how much $5,200 is to a lot of people?' When I was a kid, my parents would've had to scrimp and save and do without to come up with even $100."

Miriam Santos became immensely popular in Chicago. In the spring of 1991, both the treasurer and the mayor campaigned for office. The mayor ran for reelection, the treasurer, for her own elected term, and both won a full four-year term. In the primaries, Santos won with 69.6 percent of the vote and in the general election, she won with 71 percent of the vote, more than the mayor had received.

Santos became the first Hispanic to win a city-wide election in Chicago, and "a top prospect for higher office," according to media headlines. Obviously, she had more than just the "Hispanic vote."

As Santos said to Scott Pendleton of *The Christian Science Monitor*, "I wanted to be viewed as a capable, competent professional." Adds Pendleton, "Everyone agrees she's exactly that." As if to prove it, city funds earned more than $125 million in interest income in 1991 alone.

In the fall of 1991, a tremendous feud between Mayor Daley and City Treasurer Santos erupted in public. It began when Daley engineered a behind-the-scenes move in the legislature to change state law. The change meant that the city treasurer could be removed from the municipal pension boards. Those boards control $8 billion in investments. The mayor could now appoint anyone he wanted to sit on those boards. Daley never gave a very clear explanation of why he wanted the city treasurer removed. One thing is very clear, though: In the past, pension fund money has been loaned to political friends and allies of people in office.

Santos went into action immediately. She

called on the governor of Illinois publicly to repeal the legislature's action. "How come they do this only when there is a woman, and a Latina, in office?" she asked. "I don't think this [taking the treasurer off the boards] would benefit the taxpayers," Santos cried out. "Pension funds are partly funded by tax dollars, and having an elected official there when the investment decisions are made really brings an important level of scrutiny."

Charges and countercharges flew for weeks, but when the mayor's forces attacked Santos, they played into her hands, John Kass wrote in the *Chicago Tribune*, "enhancing her image as a woman who was tapped by Daley to reform the treasurer's office but is now being beaten up by his aides for doing just that."

In November, the governor of Illinois, Jim Edgar, vetoed the legislation that would have removed the city treasurer from the pension boards. "I tried to separate the personality dispute," Edgar explained. "I don't want to get into the middle of that. I don't know Ms. Santos. I know the mayor. He's a friend of mine. But I felt governmentally it was the wrong thing to do."

State Senator Miguel del Valle commented, "I think the real winners in this process are not Miriam Santos, the Hispanic community, the governor, or any other individual. I think the real winners are the retirees, the individuals who worked all their lives who are dependent on their pensions."

In 1992, there was speculation about Santos running for Congress. "If Miriam Santos decides to run, it's a whole different ball of wax," said Joseph N. Gómez, vice president of Mid-America Bank and chairman of the Illinois Hispanic Council. Santos was courted by both the Democrats and the Republicans, but didn't run.

Now the speculation is about the mayor's office. Will she run against Mayor Daley in 1995? When asked, she invariably says, "I don't know" or "I can't tell." She does say things like, "I came here to do a job and to do it exceptionally well." In an interview with Manuel Galván for *Hispanic* magazine, she said, "At some point, I'd like to move on, but I'm not walking away from this office until I make it a national model. We're almost there."

Is there anything for Miriam Santos outside work? she was asked one day. "My family," she responded quickly. "We all get together for birthdays and things like that. If there's no special occasion, somebody calls and says, 'Come for lunch, come for dinner.' We see one another at least once a month." Santos keeps lots of photographs of her parents, her brothers, her sister, her sisters-in-law, her nieces and nephews around. "My nieces and nephews, they're terrific. One day this one was learning to do addition at school," she says, pointing at a niece's picture, "and she called me to ask me how to do it. I'm the treasurer, right? I know numbers, right? I was in the middle of an important meeting . . . but I covered the telephone and helped her."

Santos looks at a picture of her parents, and says, "When things get crazy around here, I take a few days off and go see my parents. Then when I come back, things are fine. They bring me back to reality. My family is my support system."

The treasurer of the city of Chicago was an invited guest at the inauguration of President Bill Clinton in 1993. On this occasion, no doubt Miriam Santos thought of Ana and Manolín Santos, who toiled in the mainland, far from their Puerto Rican home, so their children could have more opportunities to succeed and achieve their potential.

10
Gloria Estefan

Gloria Estefan is quick to point out she is happy to be alive and never takes anything for granted. If she counts her blessings rather than her considerable wealth, it is understandable because she was nearly paralyzed in an accident on March 20, 1990. However, Estefan's strong will and hard work put her back on the stage as good as before, or better.

Gloria Estefan's millions were not inherited — they have been earned with talent, determin-[ation, and a little bit of luck. She was born in Havana, Cuba, on September 1, 1958, the daughter of Gloria and José Manuel Fajardo, a schoolteacher and a motorcycle policeman, respectively. She was named Gloria María and was called Glorita to distinguish her from her mother.

The salaries of a schoolteacher and a policeman

made the Fajardos a middle-class family, not rich
but not poor, either. They lived comfortably until
an event changed life in Cuba. Fidel Castro and
his followers toppled the government of Fulgen-
cio Batista on January 1, 1959.

José Manuel Fajardo's assignment as a motorcycle policeman was in the escort detail of Batista's wife. Anyone who had any connection to
the Batista regime was in jeopardy. Anyone who
did not approve of Castro was in jeopardy. The
Fajardos thought it best to leave their country as
soon as possible. They were part of the Cuban
exodus that went on through the early 1960s.
Glorita was less than two years old when the family arrived in the United States.

In Miami, Florida, where the majority of Cuban
exiles settled, Fajardo soon got involved with
other Batista supporters in what would turn out
to be a disastrous undertaking.

Castro had allied his country with the then-
Soviet Union and the United States had broken
off relations with Cuba. With the encouragement
of the Kennedy administration and the Central
Intelligence Agency (CIA), Batista's supporters
planned to invade Cuba and topple Castro's regime. The CIA trained the men, who called themselves *brigadistas*, and provided them with the
necessary equipment.

On April 17, 1961, some 1,400 Cuban exiles
landed at the Bay of Pigs, on the southwestern
coast of Cuba, as the "Exile Brigade 2506." They

were expecting assistance from U.S. airplanes and support from Cubans in their homeland, but neither materialized.

Four days later, the operation had failed completely. Fajardo, commander of the brigade's tank division, was one of about 1,100 *brigadistas* captured and imprisoned by Castro's forces. Fajardo's own cousin was the one who took him prisoner.

Meanwhile, in the States, without knowing English, Gloria Fajardo could not get a teaching job. She and her daughter Glorita lived in extreme poverty in a small apartment behind the Orange Bowl in Miami. They had no sheets for their beds or pots to cook the little food they could afford. Newspapers were their bed coverings, empty cans their cooking vessels.

Gloria Fajardo did the best she could but, "there was a lot of prejudice at the time" in Miami, her daughter says. All the Hispanics coming into the place all at once were too much for many people to accept. "I remember that my mom had a really tough time dealing with it [the prejudice]," Estefan has said. "I don't remember much about Cuba, but I do remember my first years here. . . . It was very difficult. I was alone in America with my mother while my father was in jail in Cuba."

Mrs. Fajardo, however, tried to keep the truth about her husband from her little girl and give her as normal a childhood as possible. Gloria Estefan remembers her fifth birthday party in par-

ticular: "I was real sad because my dad hadn't shown up. I knew where he was. But my mother kept telling me he was on the farm. So I would tell people, 'Don't tell my mom my dad's in prison. She thinks he's a farmer.' "

In order for the *brigadistas* to be let out of jail and returned to their families in Florida, the United States had to swap the men. For $53 million worth of food and medicine, Castro freed the men shortly before Christmas 1962, just a few months late for Glorita's birthday party.

Soon José Manuel Fajardo joined the U.S. Army and another military crusade. He was one of many returned *brigadistas* who joined the U.S. armed forces thinking that, if they did something for the U.S., they could later ask the U.S. to do something for Cuba. Fajardo rose to the rank of captain and volunteered to fight in the Vietnam War.

Glorita began attending school and loving it. She was fascinated with the study of language. Six months after starting school, she won an award for reading . . . in English, a new language for her. Later on, she would acquire a third language, French. Very early in her school years, she began to write poetry.

José Manuel Fajardo returned from Vietnam in 1968 a sick man, affected mentally as well as physically. It was diagnosed that he was suffering from multiple sclerosis.

The family learned, however, that Fajardo had

been exposed to the defoliant Agent Orange during his two years in Vietnam. Agent Orange was a chemical product used to strip trees of their leaves, to kill plant life. The United States used it in Vietnam so the Viet Cong would not find cover in the forest.

Many of the people exposed to Agent Orange have become ill from the chemical's toxic effects. Mrs. Fajardo fought the U.S. government for a full-pension for her ailing husband. She was able to prove the connection between his illness and his military service and won the case. Meanwhile, José Manuel Fajardo's deterioration continued.

By this time, Gloria Fajardo had already passed the qualifying exams to become a teacher and was teaching in a Miami school. Glorita had helped her a lot with the English language. Now Mrs. Fajardo could afford to send Glorita to Our Lady of Lourdes, a Catholic high school.

But with her mother out of the house for a good many hours of the day, Glorita had to shoulder a lot of responsibility at home. Her father had become completely paralyzed and dependent on others.

"I took care of Dad from the time I was eleven until I was sixteen," Gloria Estefan remembers. "I looked so much older [then] than I do now because I was carrying the weight of the whole world on my shoulders," Estefan says. There was also a younger little girl to look after, Rebecca, who was born after Fajardo's return from jail in

Cuba. "I was handling a lot, trying to be strong for my mom, and I was kind of like my sister's mom."

Gloria María Fajardo was a straight-A student in high school in spite of the difficulties at home. She was shy, quiet, and withdrawn in manner and a "little chubby" in appearance. After school, she always went home and once her chores were done, she would go to her room and play the guitar and sing.

"I was holding onto my emotions so much that I wouldn't cry. Instead I just sang," Estefan says. "Music was just my own thing, my personal thing that I loved."

With her guitar and her songs, Glorita Fajardo could express all the pain she felt inside. She sang the Top 40 tunes she'd learn listening to the radio, and repeated the ballads she'd heard her mother sing over the years.

José Manuel Fajardo had to be moved to the Veterans Administration hospital when Glorita was sixteen. He remained there until his death in 1980. His oldest daughter no longer had to take care of him, but she went to the hospital daily and fed her father his dinner.

The young woman still helped with other chores at home, and helped take care of her sister, but she now had time to give guitar lessons and earn a little money.

It was about then that Glorita first saw a young Cuban by the name of Emilio Estefan, Jr. He was invited to Our Lady of Lourdes High School to talk about music to the students. The young man had a full-time job in marketing with Bacardi Imports. In his spare time, he played with a group he had formed in 1974, the Miami Latin Boys. Estefan, who at age thirteen had left Cuba with his father, had a very good head for business.

Following Estefan's example, Glorita Fajardo and several of her girlfriends thought of putting together a group to entertain at a family birthday party. The father of one of her friends worked at Bacardi and asked Estefan to help the girls.

"They brought Emilio over to give us some pointers on putting a band together because he had already had a band," Gloria Estefan recalls. "Anyway, he heard me sing there, and that was it." They didn't see each other again for some time, even though they were in the same town.

Gloria María Fajardo's grades were good enough to get a scholarship to attend the University of Miami. She majored in psychology and communications and graduated at the very top of her class. While still in college, she worked for the Department of Immigration as an interpreter and translator. She liked the job and planned to make interpreting and translating her career.

One day in 1975, the Fajardos attended a wedding. Young Gloria didn't want to go. "My mother had to drag me [to the wedding]," she says. That day was a turning point in her life, one that would make her change her career plans. The Miami

Latin Boys were entertaining at the party. Emilio Estefan, their leader, was there playing the accordion.

"We ran into each other during the band's break and he [Emilio Estefan] recognized me," Gloria Estefan recalls. "He approached me and asked if I would sing a couple of numbers with the band for fun." The shy young woman was hesitant to do it, but Estefan persisted and her mother prodded her and she sang.

There were many groups like the Miami Latin Boys in the 1970s in south Florida. They sang at weddings, anniversaries, birthday parties, and other parties.

When Glorita Fajardo and Emilio Estefan met this time, the Miami Latin Boys had no lead singer. All the bands had male vocalists — but why couldn't they have a female? Emilio Estefan asked himself. He invited Glorita Fajardo to join the group within weeks of their meeting at the wedding.

Glorita Fajardo, however, said she was busy with her college studies and didn't have the time. Emilio Estefan called her again and told her she would only have to work on weekends and vacations, that this would be "like a hobby." "Well, I loved music so much that I couldn't let an opportunity like this pass me by," Gloria Estefan recalls.

Before the eighteen-year-old could consider the job, her family had to make sure the people she'd work with were acceptable. Glorita's mother and grandmother asked questions of anyone who knew the young men. They found out that they were all Cuban-born and came from nice families. Emilio Estefan was five years older than Glorita and the others were her age or a year older. Her mother agreed that she could take the job. Merci Fajardo, Glorita's cousin, also joined the band later on.

The musicians were not happy about singing with a girl. They knew of too many cases where a newly discovered "talent" sang with a band and it turned out to be a disaster. But when they heard these two young women singing together, they did not complain. Both young women were hired after their first tryout session.

Within months, Emilio Estefan's band dominated the party scene in Miami. The Fajardo cousins made all the difference. But the group's name, Miami Latin Boys, was not reflective of the band's composition anymore. Someone suggested a new name: Miami Sound Machine. Gloria Estefan recalls that she didn't like the word "machine," but others did, and the name stuck.

The Miami Sound Machine musicians belonged to what has been called the "bridge generation." They were born in Cuba but came to the United States when they were very young. They grew up with a mixture of Cuban and mainstream American customs and tastes. In music, they leaned toward American pop, rock, and jazz. But they had to entertain an older generation that preferred other types of music.

The young musicians had to learn the styles of
Tito Puente, Celia Cruz, and most of the Latin
favorites to play for their Cuban and other Hispanic patrons. They also learned old American
standards for their Anglo customers. They never
played anything original.

Glorita Fajardo and Emilio Estefan worked
very well together and gradually became attracted to each other. She thought he, being five
years older, was not paying any attention to her
as a woman. Besides, he had too many dates.
Emilio Estefan thought she was very beautiful.
He told his mother, "I am not going to make a
move on this girl unless I am serious. She's been
through too much."

Although Emilio Estefan was, and still is, a
"real flirt," he said nothing to the young singer
until July 4, 1976. That was a day for a lot of
celebrations — the U.S. Bicentennial — and
Miami Sound Machine was playing at a party on
a ship. During a break, Emilio Estefan and Glorita Fajardo went onto the top deck. He told her
he wanted her to kiss him because it was his
birthday (it was not). After that they began dating, but they were not in a rush to marry because
they wanted to make sure they were right for each
other.

In 1978, after graduating from college, the
young woman, no longer "Glorita" but Gloria
María Fajardo, joined MSM full time. Though she
was still somewhat in the background, she was
already thinking of herself as a performer and

worked very hard. Her shyness, however, was still in the way. "It was a painful process for me," Gloria Estefan says. "I really didn't get to the forefront of the band until 1982."

In 1978, the band produced its first record, titled *Miami Sound Machine*. In 1979 it produced *MSM Imported* and early in 1980, *MSM*. All three had Spanish songs on one side and English songs on the other. The records were produced in Miami for very little money.

Two years after they started dating, Emilio Estefan, Jr., and Gloria María Fajardo were sure they wanted to spend the rest of their lives with each other. They got married on September 1, 1978.

The couple who had entertained at so many weddings had a very small wedding for themselves — without a band, without a big reception! They used the money they had saved for a honeymoon in Japan. According to Emilio, that's what they should do because they would not be able to take a vacation for a long time. "He was right," she says now.

Also in 1978, Gloria Estefan made her only trip to Cuba since her family had fled the country. José Estefan, Emilio's older brother, had not been able to leave when the rest of the Estefans left. He had been drafted into the army when he reached military service age. Now José Estefan wanted to leave, but Castro's government did not allow people to leave the country easily. Anyone who planned to was treated very harshly.

Castro's people found out about José Estefan's plans two months before he and his wife and children were to depart. "Their life was made very difficult and reprisals at work and school made them go into hiding until the day of their flight," Gloria Estefan says. "We had to take them clothing and food to live on for the two months."

Gloria Estefan did not like the atmosphere in Cuba. The trip reinforced her anticommunist feelings.

Estefan has promised never to perform in Cuba, even though her music is popular there, while Castro is in power. Performing in her native land would be a betrayal of her father. Other than those statements, she refuses to be involved in politics. Politics is a very personal matter, she says.

Long-time "Gloria watchers" have noticed that her physical appearance and her personality have changed. When she started with Miami Latin Boys she was a chubby, shy girl who played maracas in the background and only came to the front when it was her turn to sing a song. Today, she is the slim energy-charged singer and dancer who never leaves the forefront during a Miami Sound Machine appearance.

While Gloria Fajardo and Emilio Estefan were dating, she began to reshape herself physically through exercise. He used to tease her about improving herself "95 percent." She thought he meant losing weight, but he really meant she could be less shy, more assertive. Her physical change, however, brought the personality changes Emilio was talking about.

In 1980, the couple had a son, Nayib Estefan. Although Gloria Estefan adores her son — "he is more important to me than anything in the whole wide world" — she never thought of quitting her music career.

"I don't feel that you're supposed to give up your career for your children," Estefan says. "When you give up something of yourself, you're usually not as happy as you were before. And if you're not happy with yourself, it's very hard to make someone else happy."

While Nayib has grown up inside the recording studios and stage arenas, his grandmother and his aunt and Emilio's aunts and cousins have always been available for him in addition to his natural parents.

In 1980, Emilio Estefan quit his successful job at Bacardi Imports to devote himself full time to Miami Sound Machine. Shortly thereafter, he secured a recording contract with Discos CBS International, part of the entertainment giant that promotes Latin artists in Latin America and elsewhere.

By 1984, the band had gotten its distinctive "Latin Miami" sound. That sound was carefully crafted to appeal to the tastes of all Hispanic groups. Many of the songs they were performing were composed by Gloria Estefan, who had written poetry since her high school days, and other members of the band.

MSM was playing to crowds of 3,000 to 4,000 people in their home area but it attracted crowds of 30,000 and 40,000 people in Latin America. In Mexico, Peru, Venezuela, Argentina, Brazil, Honduras, and Panama, they became the number one music group.

In 1982, Gloria's cousin Merci and her husband left the band. Gloria Estefan moved to the forefront of the band permanently. In the 1980s, MSM traveled extensively throughout Latin America and its financial success was enormous. But still, in the U.S. the group was not well known outside its home area.

In 1984, band member Enrique "Kiki" García wrote a song called "Dr. Beat." The words were in English and the music had a definite Latin beat. Gloria Estefan, who routinely translated everything they sang in English into Spanish, thought that this song could not be translated. Emilio Estefan decided to ask the record company to record it only in English. The record company did not want to do it because the group was identified as a Spanish-speaking group.

The company finally agreed and "Dr. Beat" was recorded on the B side of a single record, with a song in Spanish on the A side. Soon "Dr. Beat" caught fire with English-speaking disc jockeys.

The same year, 1984, MSM did its first English language album, *Eyes of Innocence*, on Epic Records, another branch of CBS Records with a worldwide marketing area. In 1985, the album *Primitive Love*, which contained the song

"Conga," became a trademark signature in every Estefan concert.

"Conga" is one of the more "Latin-sounding" pieces the band plays and it makes people dance everywhere.

It was the song "Conga" that first appeared on the dance, pop, Latin, and black charts of *Billboard* magazine at the same time. No other Latin group had ever reached that milestone. The group now became known as Gloria Estefan and the Miami Sound Machine.

The so-called crossover had been achieved. The Pepsi-Cola company used MSM music for a commercial. The movies *Top Gun*, *Cobra*, *Stakeout*, and *Three Men and a Baby* used MSM music on their soundtracks. The term "crossover" is often used in the U.S. to refer to artists who are considered part of a group or trend, and then become popular in another.

In 1987, when the group released its album *Let It Loose*, Emilio Estefan quit playing in the band. He became a producer full time. Now, for the first time, Gloria Estefan traveled with the band but Emilio stayed home with Nayib. After that, the boy and his father would travel with her sometimes but not always, as they had done before.

In 1988, Gloria Estefan won the Broadcast Music International Songwriter of the Year award, and she and MSM won the American Music Award for Best Pop/Rock Group of the Year; MSM was named the second most popular group in the U.S. by *Billboard* magazine; Emilio Estefan was

nominated as Best Producer of the Year for an
American Music Award.

In the same year, Enrique "Kiki" García quit
Miami Sound Machine. Of the original band, only
Gloria Estefan remained.

In 1989, the album *Cuts Both Ways* was released. The tour that year played to sold-out
crowds in England, Scotland, Holland, and Belgium. Late in 1989, while touring the U.S., Gloria
Estefan got influenza but kept singing even with
a bad sore throat. She did some damage to her
vocal chords and the tour had to be cut short
because the doctor ordered her home to recuperate.

By January 1990, Gloria Estefan was back on
the road. Early in March, CBS Records gave Gloria Estefan and Miami Sound Machine the Crys-
tal Globe Award. It is given to artists who sell
five million records or more outside their home
country.

On March 19, 1990, the Estefans went to the
White House in Washington, D.C. President
George Bush invited them so he could thank
Gloria Estefan personally for her antidrug campaign, in which her picture appeared on bill-
boards saying, "If you need someone, call a
friend. Don't do drugs." The next day they headed
for a concert in Syracuse, New York. Emilio
wanted to fly there, but Gloria preferred to travel
in their rented customized bus whenever she
could. On the bus she could rest and be refreshed
for the show, she said.

It was sunny when Gloria Estefan went to sleep on a couch in the bus on March 20. Emilio Estefan was conducting business on the phone. Nayib was in the back of the bus studying with his tutor. When Gloria Estefan woke up later, along a Pennsylvania interstate highway, it was dark and snowing and the bus had stopped due to an accident ahead. Traffic was totally halted, waiting for the road to be cleared.

A few minutes later, at 12:15 P.M., a truck slammed into the Estefans' bus from behind. It was "like an explosion," they said. "There were no seat belts on the bus, and I must have been thrown off the couch, because the next thing that I remember is lying on my back on the floor in excruciating pain," Gloria Estefan told an interviewer. "I had the strangest taste in my mouth, almost electrical, and I knew instantly I had broken my back."

Before Emilio could answer Gloria's anguished "What happened?" the truck that hit them the first time slammed into the bus a second time. The bus slammed into the truck in front of it. The driver's side collapsed completely but the driver was not killed because he had moved away from his seat to help Emilio after the first jolt.

Others in the bus were injured but none as seriously as the star. Nayib had a broken collarbone. Emilio, the bus driver, and a secretary had minor injuries. The ambulance arrived a full hour after the accident and it took forty-five minutes to get to the Regional Trauma Center of the

Scranton Community Medical Center.

Gloria Estefan's self-diagnosis was correct; two of the vertebrae in the middle of her spine were fractured. "Another half-inch of movement of the spine," said Dr. Harry Schmaltz in Scranton, "and she'd be completely paralyzed."

There was a choice of two treatments for this type of injury. One was putting the person in a body cast for six months to let the bones knit by themselves. There was almost no hope of a complete recovery with this type of treatment.

The other treatment was spinal surgery. With surgery, there was the risk of an infection and, beyond that, permanent paralysis. But the operation would permit the doctors to see the extent of the damage, and it was possible the damage could be repaired. Gloria Estefan decided on the surgery.

"I didn't want the doctors in Scranton to feel I didn't trust them, but I wanted a surgeon who did this operation daily," says Gloria Estefan. So Emilio called all over the country and finally they decided that Dr. Michael Neuwirth, at the Hospital for Joint Diseases in New York City, should do the operation.

Dr. Neuwirth brought Gloria Estefan from Scranton to New York City by helicopter. "The way she tolerates the pain!" said the doctor to the reporters waiting at the hospital. "Riding in a helicopter with a broken back for forty-five minutes must have been uncomfortable. There was not a peep of complaint."

The doctor inserted one eight-inch stainless steel rod on each side of the spine, which will remain permanently in Gloria Estefan's back. They support the broken vertebrae and relieve the pressure on her spinal nerves. Next the doctor inserted bone taken from the pelvic area, ground up, so that it will eventually fuse with the broken vertebrae to form a stiff band of bone around the steel rods.

The Estefans take the steel rods with humor nowadays. Gloria says that Emilio calls her "RoboCop," and tells her she should carry her X rays with her. That way, when she goes through the metal detector machines at the airport and they ring, she can show why.

The operation, on March 22, took four hours to complete; the incision was fourteen inches long and was closed with more than 400 stitches. That evening, Dr. Neuwirth announced that, given the success of the operation, Gloria Estefan could expect to regain 95 to 100 percent of her mobility.

The outpouring of affection was astonishing. Estefan received calls and visits from numerous big stars. President Bush called her twice. TV stations and newspapers from all over the world sent reporters to the hospital. She received four thousand flower arrangements and more than forty-eight thousand cards. She distributed the flowers among other patients at the hospital, in the AIDS ward, and in the nearby Veterans Administration hospital.

On April 4, Gloria Estefan returned to Miami.

She arrived on Julio Iglesias's personal jet. The
Spanish singer, a close friend of the Estefans, sent
the plane to bring her back home to recuperate.
Gloria Estefan walked off the plane on her own,
leaning lightly on her husband's arm. She
thanked the crowd, waving and smiling. No one
could imagine the pain that she had had to endure
on the plane.

Gloria Estefan immediately started the most
intensive physical exercise program of her life —
six hours a day. "She was in pain so much of the
time," her husband says, "but she never complained. Not once." Estefan was determined to
be back on the stage. She knew it was possible
because Joe Montana had recovered fully from
very serious injuries and had returned to the football field. "I wouldn't want to get back on that
stage and be less than I was. I'm trying to even
go beyond what I did before," she said then.

During the time of her recuperation, Gloria Estefan wrote more songs. Those songs would be
the basis for her new album and a worldwide
tour. She also made a film appearance at Jerry
Lewis's Labor Day Telethon for the Muscular
Dystrophy Association in September 1990. Estefan said then that she felt better, and luckier,
every day, that she knew her full recovery needed
hard work but she was never afraid of hard work.

In January 1991, Gloria Estefan appeared at
the American Music Awards. She danced, she
sang, and she was ready to launch a tour to promote her new album, *Into the Light*. The album

starts with the song "Coming Out of the Dark." It also has "Nayib's Song," subtitled "I am here for you."

On March 1, 1991, Gloria Estefan sang and danced in an incredible performance before a home crowd in Miami. Then she went on tour around the world and did 130 shows. Her elaborate productions required 2,000 pounds of equipment (lights, microphones, costumes, sets, etc.), ten buses and trucks, and a crew of at least 100 persons.

On March 20, 1991, one year to the date after the accident, Estefan's song "Coming Out of the Dark" went up to number one on the charts.

In 1992, after the Hurricane Andrew devastation in Florida, the Estefans organized a relief effort with the help of many celebrity friends. The one-night show raised almost $2 million. Then Gloria Estefan recorded a ballad she had recently written, "Always Tomorrow," and all the money from it was earmarked for victims of the hurricane.

"I owe these people so much," says Estefan. "After all, they were there for me when I had the accident. They went out to their churches and synagogues and prayed for me. They didn't even know me personally, but they sent me cards and were really good to me."

In May 1992, in Las Vegas, Gloria Estefan received a lifetime achievement award ("Premio lo Nuestro") from an organization devoted to Latin music. Later that year, in September, the city of

Miami honored the Estefans for their contribution to Miami's image. That was only the most
recent honor they have been given in their home
town.

Other honors include the naming of the street
where they live Miami Sound Machine Boulevard, and several awards from the Chamber of
Commerce, as representatives of the new bilingual, multicultural city Miami is today. For her
part, Gloria Estefan has said, "I don't feel Cuban.
I don't feel American. I feel 'Latin Miami.' "

More recently, Gloria Estefan has started work
with the United Nations as a "public delegate."
No doubt, she will be involved in many human-
itarian projects in years to come. She has her own
good example to follow.

The first all-Spanish album recorded by Gloria
Estefan, *Mi Tierra* [*My Homeland*], was released
in 1993 and it won her a Grammy award. The
songs are all original and the music takes ele-
ments from numerous Afro-Cuban rhythms and
styles. Some of the biggest names in Latin music,
such as Tito Puente, perform on this recording.
One of the songs challenges Hispanics from various countries who now live in the United States
to forget their regional differences and be united
as Latinos.

The Estefans run a successful business — Estefan Enterprises. They own the building where
the business is located and a big state-of-the-art
recording studio in Miami. Emilio Estefan pro-

duces not only his wife's records but the records of other artists as well.

Gloria Estefan has performed for the Prince of Wales, the Prince of Spain, the President of the Philippines, and the President of the United States. She was the first to leave her footprints on "Star Boulevard," a place to honor artists in Scheveningen, Holland.

She could very well afford to stay home and do nothing. But she keeps working as hard as ever and traveling everywhere because she loves what she does. One thing, though: Gloria Estefan never travels in a vehicle without seat belts.

Selected Bibliography and Sources

David G. Farragut

Farragut, Loyall. *The Life of David Glasgow Farragut, First Admiral of the United States Navy.* New York: D. Appleton and Company, 1879.

Fernández-Shaw, Carlos M. "David G. Farragaut: First Admiral of the United States." In *Hispanic Presence in the United States*, edited by Frank de Varona. Miami: The National Hispanic Quincentennial Commission/Mnemosyne Publishing Company, 1993.

Mahan, A. T. *Admiral Farragut.* New York: D. Appleton and Company, 1892.

Porter, David D. *The Naval History of the Civil War.* New York: The Sherman Publishing Company, 1886.

Shorto, Russell. *David Farragut and the Great Naval Blockade.* Englewood Cliffs, NJ: Silver Burdett Press, 1991.

Sinnott, Susan. *Extraordinary Hispanic Americans*. Chicago: Children's Press, 1991.

U.S. Naval Institute. *David Glasgow Farragut, Our First Admiral*. Annapolis, MD: U.S. Naval Institute, 1943.

Wolford, Tonya E. "Fighting for Freedom: David Glasgow Farragut," *Hispanic*, May 1991.

Severo Ochoa

Biographical Encyclopedia of Scientists, vol 2. New York: Facts-on-File, 1981.

Kornberg, A., B. L. Horecker, L. Cornudella & J. Oró (editors). *Reflections on Biochemistry. In Honour of Severo Ochoa*. Oxford, England: Pergamon Press, 1976.

Kornberg, Arthur. *For the Love of Enzymes*. Cambridge, MA: Harvard University Press, 1989.

Nachmanson, David. *German-Jewish Pioneers in Science 1900–1933*. Berlin: Springer-Verlag, 1976.

Schlessinger, Bernard S. and June H. Schlessinger (editors). *The Who's Who of Nobel Prize Winners 1901–1990*. Phoenix, AZ: Oryx Press, 1991.

Wasson, Tyler (editor). *Nobel Prize Winners*. The H. W. Wilson Company, 1987.

Jaime Escalante

American Association of School Administrators. "Educators' Group Honors Escalante," *Los Angeles Times*, February 25, 1990.

Aparicio, Yvette. "We Stood and Delivered, as TV

Stared," *The Christian Science Monitor*, July 31, 1990.

Barry, Paul. "Strong Medicine. A Talk With Former Principal Henry Gradillas," *The College Board Review*, no. 153, Fall 1989.

Escalante, J. and J. Dirman. "Jaime Escalante Math Program," *Journal of Negro Education* 59, 3, Summer 1990.

Escalante, Jaime. Interview with author, March 1993.

Fajardo, Angela. "Motivation Is the Key," *Los Angeles Times*, October 14, 1991.

Mathews, Jay. *Escalante: The Best Teacher in America*. New York: Henry Holt and Company, 1988.

Meek, Anne. "On Creating *Ganas*: A Conversation With Jaime Escalante," *Educational Leadership*, February 1989.

Savage, David. "Don't Tell Jaime Escalante Minorities Can't Meet (High) Standards," *Instructor* (California Special Issue), Spring 1986.

Sellers, Leonard. "Can This Man Save American Education?" *Connoisseur*, April 1990.

Warner Brothers. *Stand and Deliver* (film). 1988.

Roberto Clemente

Bjarkman, Peter C. *Roberto Clemente*. New York: Chelsea House, 1991.

Kaplan, Jim. "It's a Dream Come True. Roberto Clemente's Sports City Is Taking Shape," *Sports Illustrated*, October 5, 1987.

Musick, Phil. *Who Was Roberto? A Biography of*

Roberto Clemente. Garden City, NY: Doubleday and Co., 1974.

New York Newsday, December 26, 1992. "In Memory of Roberto Clemente," reprinted from *Los Angeles Times.*

Oleksak, Michael M. and Mary Adams Oleksak. *Béisbol: Latin Americans and the Grand Old Game.* Grand Rapids, MI: Masters Press, 1991.

Rodríguez-Mayoral, Luis. *Roberto Clemente aún escucha las ovaciones.* Carolina, P. R.: Ciudad Deportiva Roberto Clemente, 1987.

Wagenheim, Kal. *Clemente!* New York: Praeger, 1973.

Walker, Paul Robert. *Pride of Puerto Rico: The Life of Roberto Clemente.* San Diego: Harcourt Brace Jovanovich, 1988.

Vilma S. Martínez

Benavidez, Max. "Vilma Martínez: Portrait of a Fighter," *Equal Opportunity Forum,* March 1982.

Codye, Corinn. *Vilma Martínez.* Austin, TX: Steck-Vaughn Company, 1991.

Dewey, Katrina M. "Profile: Vilma S. Martínez, Partner, Munger, Tolles & Olson," *Los Angeles Daily Journal,* January 9, 1992.

Enríquez, Sam. "Vilma Martínez: *Regente con misión importante.*/UC Policy-Maker With a Mission: Vilma Martínez," *Los Angeles Times,* February 9, 1987.

Hernández, Al Carlos. "Vilma Martínez, una

chicana ejemplar," *Nuestro*, August/September 1981.

Johnson, Dean. "Chair of the Board" (interview with Vilma Martínez, chair of the University of California Board of Regents), *Nuestro*, September 1985.

MALDEF 1978/ MALDEF Diez Años. A Report.

Martínez, Vilma. Interview with author, March 1993.

"Vilma Martínez. Attorney Leads Professional and Public Life of Achievement and Fulfillment," *Hispanic Community Magazine*, April/May 1988.

Antonia C. Novello

"Antonia C. Novello, U.S. Surgeon General," *Biography Today 1992 Annual Cumulation*. Detroit, MI: Omnigraphics, Inc., 1993.

Current Biography Yearbook 1992. New York: The H. W. Wilson Company, 1993.

Grier, Rosey. *Rosey Grier's All-American Heroes*. New York: Master Media Ltd., 1993.

Jones, Laurie. "Surgeon General Sees Self as Positive Role Model," *American Medical News*, April 27, 1990.

Krucoff, Carol. "Antonia Novello: A Dream Come True," *The Saturday Evening Post*, May/June 1991.

"Meet: The Country's Doctor," *NEA Today*, February 1992.

Novello, Antonia. Interview with author, February 1993.

————. "Beyond Statistics," *Hispanic*, January/February 1991.

————. "Health Priorities for the Nineties," *Vital Speeches of Our Time*. Speech delivered at the Town Hall of California, Los Angeles, California, April 21, 1992.

Franklin R. Chang-Díaz

"A Giant Leap Forward," *Nuestro*, January/February 1986.

Browne, Malcolm W. "A Dreamer in Space — Franklin R. Chang-Díaz," *The New York Times*, January 13, 1986.

Chang-Díaz, Franklin R. Interview with author, December 1992.

Germani, Clara. "Chang-Díaz: From Spotting *Sputnik* to Flying the Shuttle," *The Christian Science Monitor*, January 3, 1984.

Graf, Gary R. "The Plasma Drive from Costa Rica," *Space World*, June 1986.

NASA. "61-C Spacecraft Tour and VIP Phone Call/Chang-Díaz, Payload Specialist" (video).

O'Toole, Thomas. "Hispanic Astronaut Trades Dream for the Real Stuff," *The Washington Post*, January 18, 1986.

Pena, Silvia Novo. "The Next Frontier: Hispanics in the Space Program," *Hispanic*, January/February 1989.

Fernando Bujones

Barnes, Patricia. Personal notes, 1991.

Bujones, Fernando. Interview with author, 1992.

Fanger, Iris M. "On the Road to Boston," *Dance*, May 1991.

Gernand, Renèe. *The Cuban Americans*. New York: Chelsea House, 1988.

Kultur. *Fernando Bujones in* Coppelia (video) 1980.

Shapiro, Laura. "A 'Swan Lake' Made in Heaven," *Newsweek*, May 14, 1990.

Unterburger, Amy L. (editor). *Who's Who Among Hispanic Americans, 1991–92*, first edition. Detroit, MI: Gale Research Associates, 1991.

Miriam Santos

Adachi, Christina. "Miriam Santos: Making Dollars & Sense Out of City Hall" (cover story), *Today's Chicago Woman*, May 1992.

Díaz, Katharine A. "Miriam Santos: Chicago's Latina Treasurer," *Hispanic American Family*, Winter 1989.

Galván, Manuel. "No Small Change" (cover story), *Hispanic*, May 1992.

Klages, Karen E. "Terminator, Too. City Treasurer Miriam Santos Gives the Politicians a Run for Their Money." (cover story), Style, *Chicago Tribune*, December 11, 1991.

Roman, Ivan. "Daley Winds Up in Loser's Corner in Slugfest With Chicago Treasurer," *Miami Herald*, August 9, 1992.

Santos, Miriam. Interview with author, January 1993.

Secter, Bob. "Pension Dispute Latest Windy City

Political Intrigue," *Los Angeles Times*, November 7, 1991.

Gloria Estefan

Cocks, Jay. "Dancing on the Charts," *Time*, May 28, 1990.

Coto, Juan Carlos. "1-2-3 With Gloria," *Miami Herald*, September 7, 1988.

Estefan, Gloria (as told to Kathryn Casey). "My Miracle," *Ladies Home Journal*, August 1990.

Gifford, Susan Korones. "Red Hot Right Now: Gloria Estefan, a Sound Machine Again," *Cosmopolitan*, June 1991.

Gloria Estefan Into the Light. Sony Music Video, 1991.

Gloria Estefan Coming Out of the Dark. Sony Music Video, 1991.

McGovern, Michael. "Miami-based Singer Gloria Estefan Is Carving Her Own World as Philanthropist and Public Servant," *New York Daily News*, November 11, 1992.

Index

About the Author

ARGENTINA PALACIOS was born in Panama and has lived in the United States since 1961. She taught Spanish in Austin, Texas, before moving to New York City, where she now resides. She has worked as an editor for several major publishing houses, including Scholastic Inc.

In addition to her editorial work, Argentina Palacios has translated almost one hundred children's books from English into Spanish. She is also a professional storyteller.

Books for young people written or co-authored by Argentina Palacios include *The Knight and the Squire*, *This Can Lick a Lollipop/Esto puede chupar un caramelo* (with Joel Rothman), *Globe Hispanic Biographies* (with Alfredo Bejar and Steven Otfinoski), *¡Viva México!*, *¿Quién llama?*, *The Hummingbird King*, *The Llama's Secret*, and *A Christmas Surprise for Chabelita*. She has also written numerous stories for textbooks in English and in Spanish.